Audrey kissed him

Brian froze. Her soft, warm lips pressed against his and short-circuited his brain, sending an electric charge through his skin. He wanted more, he wanted all of her, with an urgency that stole his breath, but he also recognized the kiss for what it was.

A gesture of gratitude and relief.

And he would have had to be the worst kind of bastard to take advantage of it. Brian pulled back and saw surprise flicker in her eyes before he looked away. Surprise at her own spontaneous gesture or at his reaction.

It didn't matter. He wasn't going there.

He couldn't.

DANA MARTON
CAMOUFLAGE HEART

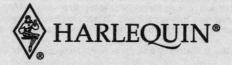

HARLEQUIN®

TORONTO • NEW YORK • LONDON
AMSTERDAM • PARIS • SYDNEY • HAMBURG
STOCKHOLM • ATHENS • TOKYO • MILAN • MADRID
PRAGUE • WARSAW • BUDAPEST • AUCKLAND

To Kim Nadelson, a wonderful editor and dear friend.

Acknowledgments:

With many thanks to Allison Lyons, Jenel Looney and Anita Staley for their help and support. And with much appreciation to my family and friends for not minding that writing is all I talk about and for cheering me on. Pat and Ariff, thank you for sharing your vast knowledge of Malaysia. All mistakes are my own.

ISBN 0-373-88649-7

CAMOUFLAGE HEART

ABOUT THE AUTHOR

Dana Marton lives near Wilmington, Delaware. She has been an avid reader since childhood and has a master's degree in writing popular fiction. When not writing, she can be found either in her garden or her home library. For more information on the author and her other novels, please visit her Web site at www.danamarton.com.

She would love to hear from her readers via e-mail: DanaMarton@yahoo.com.

Books by Dana Marton

HARLEQUIN INTRIGUE
806—SHADOW SOLDIER
821—SECRET SOLDIER
859—THE SHEIK'S SAFETY
875—CAMOUFLAGE HEART

CAST OF CHARACTERS

Audrey Benedict—When her sister is kidnapped by Malaysian guerillas, she rushes to pay the ransom money, but is captured.

Brian Welkins—Member of a top secret military group (SDDU). Four years ago, he was captured by the guerillas and kept in a cage since. All he wanted was to escape and get as far from the jungle as possible. And then Audrey came along.

Nicky Benedict-Sawyer—She came to Malaysia on an adoption trip to provide moral support to her sister, Audrey. But a simple sightseeing excursion to the island of Borneo ended in disaster.

Jamil—Once a true freedom fighter, now he leads a small guerilla group that's becoming increasingly difficult to control.

Omar—Jamil's younger brother who thinks it's past time he took charge and led the group to fight.

Hamid—Head of the group that took twelve Western hostages. But the kidnappings are not his worst crime. He has plans for the ransom money that will send shockwaves through the region.

SDDU—Special Designation Defense Unit. A top secret military team established to fight terrorism. Its existence is known only by a select few. Members are recruited from the best of the best.

Colonel Wilson—Brian's boss. He's the leader of the SDDU, reporting straight to the Homeland Security Secretary.

Chapter One

Soon.

Don't act strange. Don't draw attention. Don't even look alive.

Brian hid his shaking hands under his arms. He had spent the last four years waiting for a chance to escape, but now that the opportunity was here it overwhelmed him. He took a slow breath. He was in better shape than he'd been at any of his previous attempts. Which still didn't guarantee that he could break out of his prison and make the two-week trek out of the Malaysian jungle.

"We'll be back in three days, four at the most," Jamil, the guerilla group's leader, said to his younger brother on the other side of the clearing, the tension obvious between the two men even from a distance.

The steadily pattering rain drowned out the younger man's reply. The mesh of banana leaves Brian had woven among the top bars of the tiger cage leaked here and there, but the makeshift roof kept the worst of the weather off him. He watched his captors from the corner of his eye, keeping his head turned toward the trees. He didn't want them to know he was paying attention.

"Haven't you wasted enough time trying to convince everyone Hamid is wrong?" Omar raised his voice and could be heard now even over the rain. "We've become like old women, talking around campfires. Bullets win wars, not talk." He spat the words. "We can start by sending this one's head—" he jerked his thumb toward Brian "—to the city."

Jamil lifted a placating hand. There was a presence to the older man, a careful dignity that the others lacked. "We are freedom fighters, not terrorists."

And that's where he was wrong, Brian

thought. Jamil and a couple of the older men in camp might have started out as freedom fighters, but Omar and his young friends were in this for entirely different reasons. They liked the outlaw power of bending to no government, taking what they wanted when they came across some-one weaker.

Jamil nodded to his men and disap-peared into the jungle with them. Brian stared straight ahead, not looking at the re-maining fighters, but aware of each and every one. The small guerilla group con-sisted of about three dozen men. Eight had gone for supplies two days ago. Jamil was taking six to talk alliance with a larger group on the other side of the mountain.

For the next few days, the camp would be as thin as ever, and tomorrow night Ah-mad would be on guard duty. Ahmad would let him go to the bathroom without pistol-whipping him first for the bother, or standing behind him the whole time with a rifle barrel pressed between his shoulder blades.

Just a little longer. Just another day.

Brian closed his eyes. He needed some sleep, to have as much energy as possible when the time came. The familiar noises of the jungle filled the night, the chorus of frogs interrupted now and then by the shrill cry of a bird, the buzz and chirp of a million insects filling in the occasional silence.

His mind drifted, but something prickled at the edges of his consciousness. Something was missing. The camp was quiet. Unnaturally so. No human voices joined that of the jungle. He opened his eyes.

Omar still stood on the same spot, but a dozen of his men were gathered around him. Now what? He watched as some kind of silent communication passed between them and the men melted into the jungle one by one.

Minutes passed, then came the sounds of gunfire from the distance. Some of Jamil's men jumped up and ran into the forest. Brian swore under his breath. If Omar managed to wrest leadership of the group, he was finished.

A good hour went by before the last gun fell silent, and not long after that, the first fighters returned to camp. Jamil's men were not among them.

Brian swallowed his desperation and tried to catch Ahmad's eye. If he could get the younger man to come over, let him out of the cage… But Ahmad was busy at the other end of the clearing, joining the celebration that had begun.

It didn't take much before half the camp was drunk and the other half well on their way. Brian looked up at the darkening sky. They hadn't come for him yet, but he knew Omar would get to it sooner or later. Whether or not to keep their prisoner alive had been one of the main disagreements between the brothers. Omar would want to reassert his new authority by making a point.

He had to go. Now.

"Ahmad," he called out on a low voice when the man walked near him.

The young fighter turned to see what he wanted, but then stopped, his attention drawn to a commotion at the edge of the clearing. The group that had gone off for supplies was returning.

Damn it. Not that, too.

So much for taking advantage of a sparse camp. What the hell were they doing back? The trip to the nearest kampongs, the few villages that were this high up the mountain, usually took five or six days.

And then he saw the hunched figure they were shoving in front of them.

Another prisoner.

He leaned forward to get a better look at the young man. No, not a kid—it was a woman. Definitely a woman.

She was pushed close enough to the low fire that burned under a hatch-roofed shelter, so he could see her clearly now. Her hands were bound behind her, her mouth gagged. The light of the flames glinted off blondish hair.

Jamil hadn't been keen on the practice of exchanging hostages for money. On the odd occasion when Omar's men brought back some easy target they couldn't resist, they were sent upriver to a larger guerilla group whose leader, Hamid, was an expert in this kind of business. There had been talk of a job he had recently pulled, how they were expecting the batch of hostages to bring in over a million ringgits a head.

The woman turned for a moment, and the fire lit her face enough so that he could see her eyes. They were filled with stark terror, so vivid he could feel it in his own chest.

She stirred something in him, bringing back memories, making him remember why he had joined the Special Designation Defense Unit in the first place. It used to be his job to stop this kind of thing from happening, to get to the bad guys before they got to the civilians. But he had failed.

Where the hell had Ahmad gone? Now was the time to slip away, while everyone was busy with the new prisoner.

One of the men tied the woman to a palm tree. They probably would make her write a letter to her loved ones in the morning. Then in a week or two, the money would arrive and someone would walk her to the nearest village. At least, that's how Hamid ran his deals.

He glimpsed Ahmad at last. The man had strode back to the fire and was now taking his turn from the bottle, satisfying his curiosity about the prisoner. He was too far to call to without drawing attention.

The fighters were getting louder, and Omar was busy writing on loose sheets of paper on his knee, looking up now and then when his men toasted him. Then he rolled up the papers, tied them with a piece of string and handed them to Ahmad.

This was it. Brian got to his feet and crouched—the tiger cage did not allow him to stand to his full height. He called to the young fighter as the man walked by the cage. "I need to get out for a minute."

"I'll tell one of the guards."

The two men on guard duty were at the fire with the rest, having abandoned their posts to check out the new prisoner. Jamil wouldn't have tolerated that. Omar didn't seem to notice.

"It won't take long. The others…" He let his voice trail off.

The others would beat him for the fun of it. And they were drunk enough so they might not know when to stop. Ahmad understood and stepped to the nearby post for the handcuffs, threw them into the cage. Brian slipped on the rusty metal pieces and clinked them together, hoping it sounded enough like the click that locked them. And it must have, because the door opened to let him out.

He walked in front, dragging his right foot, exaggerating the limp. He wanted anyone who watched to think he couldn't run even if his life depended on it. And it did.

He stepped a couple of feet deeper into the jungle than was necessary, made sure they were behind thick enough vegetation. He fumbled with his rope belt, let his pants drop, then spun with full force and brought his fists to Ahmad's temple. The man folded without a sound.

Brian grabbed the gun even before he pulled up his pants, "Sorry, buddy."

He pocketed Ahmad's knife, took the rolled up sheets of paper. They would come in handy once he got far enough that he could risk starting a fire. He listened, but no shouts rang out from camp, no sign that his actions were heard or seen, just the coarse jesting of the men about the woman.

As he turned to leave, he heard Omar join in. That didn't bode well for her.

A true leader knew how to rein in his men, but Omar had never been good at delayed gratification. He was too smart to intentionally kill her, but not smart enough to realize that if he let his men go at her, she probably wouldn't survive the night, and they would lose out on the ransom money.

Brian gripped the gun. He should be running right now. He should be a hundred feet away.

Ahmad groaned.

Two hundred.

He couldn't go back for her. What if she didn't speak English? She would probably fight him. He didn't look any different from the guerillas—even his clothing was the same, his original uniform having rotted off him in the jungle's humid air years ago.

She could get both of them killed. And even if he managed to get her away from camp, she would slow him down. What the hell could she know about jungle survival? She would probably keel over from the first bug that bit her. And no way to get her away unseen, either. The attention of every man in the camp was focused on her, and would probably stay on her for some time—an unexpected gift he should be taking advantage of.

And yet, he could not forget the look in her eyes.

Damn.

He pulled the man's hat off and shoved it into his mouth, tied Ahmad's hands behind his back with his belt. With a last glance at him, Brian crouched and rushed left, moving silently over the mossy ground as he circled the camp.

SHE WAS GOING to suffocate.

Audrey Benedict tried desperately to draw enough air into her burning lungs, but her mouth was taped shut, and her nose was plugged from crying.

She didn't understand a word the men around the campfire were saying, but she had no trouble interpreting their savage expressions. She had a good idea what they had in store for her. She looked up to the stars and prayed, for herself and for her sister—for someone to get to Nicky in time, now that she had failed.

She took one jerky, hard breath after another, desperate to clear her airway. An urgent shout rang across the clearing. She scanned the darkness beyond the fire, struggling against the ropes that bound her hands. The guerillas were grabbing for their guns, rushing toward a young fighter who had staggered out of the forest. Some of them ran into the jungle behind him.

Were they under attack? Dear God, let it be a rescue team and not another group of bandits.

She felt a sharp tug on her rope before it went slack, then she was yanked back through the bushes with force. She scrambled to see who or what was behind her.

If she weren't gagged, she would have screamed.

As it was, she couldn't open her mouth, and the wildman of the jungle who had her didn't leave her time to faint. He grabbed her wrist tight enough to cut off circulation and pulled her after him with frightening speed, flying through the blind night without a sound. She, on the other hand, got caught on every branch.

Her right hand was still tied to her feet, loose enough to allow movement, but not so she could reach her face. He had her other hand and wouldn't let it go, though she pulled until she thought her skin would rip off.

She was dizzy from lack of air, her ears popping. Stop! She screamed, but it came to no more than an unintelligible sound in her throat. She threw her full weight to the ground, bent head to hand, ripped the tape off her mouth.

She gulped the night air, her surroundings coming back into focus slowly. The rifle hanging from the man's shoulder knocked against her elbow as he snatched the tape from her before she could toss it. He put a finger to his lips, barely visible under a fright of a beard that came to the middle of his chest. Okay, she was supposed to be quiet. She got that.

The man pulled her up, then forward again relentlessly, and she chose to believe he was trying to help her. She preferred it to thinking she was being kidnapped again. But even if that was the case, he was only one man. She was still better off than a few minutes ago.

A creek crossed their path and he dragged her into it, moving fast from stone to stone, going downstream in the middle. The canopy was thinner here, some moonlight filtering through. She followed his movements as closely as she could, trying to stay out of the water as much as possible. She'd read about the parasites.

"Bolehkah tolong saya?" She whispered one of the few sentences she knew in Malay. *Can you help me?*

A look of surprise crossed his face before he nodded and put his fingers over her lips. She flinched away from his dirty hand and split fingernails. He didn't seem to notice her distaste and moved on, hauling her behind him.

After a few hundred yards, they reached a bend where thick vines hung into the water from the branches above. He stopped and cut off her dangling ropes, tucked them into his shirt, then turned his back to her.

"Get on," he said in English.

She hesitated a moment, but when he gave an impatient grunt, she put her arms around his neck, keeping her face from the filthy dreadlocks that streamed halfway down his back.

He bent his knees and reached under her legs with his hands, wrapped them around his waist, then let them go to reach for the vine. The rifle scraped against her side. Could she get it away from him? The sudden possibility of freedom sent blood rushing through her head. Then common sense put in an appearance and prevailed. Even with a gun, her chance of making it out of the jungle alone was uncomfortably close to zero. For one, she had no idea which way to walk.

The decision was taken from her as they were moving up, higher and higher. She didn't dare let go of him now to grab for the rifle. He was going way too fast for as dark as it was.

Freaking Tarzan. Either that or the missing link. But he spoke English and he hadn't hurt her yet. She hung on to that for hope.

Sweet heavens but he stunk.

The higher he climbed, the tighter she gripped, until he growled again, and she remembered herself and loosened her arms. If she cut off his air, they'd both fall to their death.

They reached a limb at last, and he waited until she climbed on, guiding her with one hand. Then he leaped after her, with considerably more speed and grace than she had moved. He clamped onto her wrist again—not as tight this time—and pulled her behind him as they made their way from branch to slippery branch, tree to tree. Then they stopped, and she could hear men running through the jungle below.

Her knees shook. At least it was too dark to see the ground so she could pretend they weren't all that high up. The tree canopy was one solid mass beneath them, with a fifteen-to-twenty foot gap above, then another layer of canopy that blocked out most of the sky. After a few minutes, the man next to her grabbed her and pulled her forward again.

"Where are we going?"

He ignored her and she didn't have the

wherewithal to demand an answer, needing to keep her full concentration on her
feet so she wouldn't fall.

A good hour must have passed before
they began to descend. He waited and listened before lowering her to the ground
and jumping after her.

The first thing she saw was the mouth of
a cave in front of them. Their flight from
the guerillas apparently had a destination.

It would have been nice if that destination was a village from where she could
have contacted the authorities for help, instead of a cave in the middle of the wilder-
ness, but still, at least they would be out of
the rain for a while. And maybe in the
morning she could convince the wildman
to lead her out of the jungle.

"Come on." He pulled her forward.

She followed him into the pitch-black
cave with some misgivings. Was he a her-
mit? Was he even sane? Her eyes adjusted
to the darkness slowly. The place was
about the size of her living room back
home. He led her to the back and helped
her climb the rock face.

"Is this where you live?"

"Hurry." He pointed with his head, and she spotted the ledge a good fifteen feet above. She slipped, but before she had the chance to fall, he propped her up and came after her.

The rock was covered with something soft and slippery that stunk bad enough to make her gag, the space she reached no more than a three-feet gap between the ledge and the ceiling. But it would keep them sheltered from view.

What little moonlight lit the cave didn't reach the back of the crevice where they lay side-by-side, their arms touching. When he moved away, she wanted to move after him until they touched again, needing that human contact, the knowledge that she wasn't alone in the darkness—but she didn't dare. She had no idea what to expect of him.

"Who are you?" she whispered, risking getting him mad at her for talking.

"Brian."

A normal, ordinary name, familiar. And he did speak English. She relaxed a little. "Are you American?"

"Montana."

Her lungs expanded. She tried to picture a cowboy inside the wildman but she failed. "I'm from New York. Audrey Benedict. What are you doing here?"

"The guerillas caught me a couple of years ago."

And then she remembered the large cage and something in it she hadn't been able to see because it had been too far from the fire. She'd had enough to worry about at the time to pay much attention to it. Had that been him? The horror of being kept in a cage like an animal, year in, year out, constricted her throat. God, what had they done to him? No wonder he looked barely human.

Was that what would have awaited her if he hadn't broken them out? Her insides trembled, slightly at first, then more violently. Then he found her hand in the darkness and squeezed it. In warning. She heard voices below. There were people in the cave.

She shook harder, saw light flicker above. The guerillas had a flashlight. Panic gripped her, pushing her muscles to bolt, but there was nowhere to go. An arm slid over her middle as Brian pulled her to him and held her tight in the darkness, probably only to restrain her from doing something stupid, but she didn't care. She burrowed into the comfort of the contact, curling against him like a child.

The night thundered outside, the rain coming in a downpour now, drowning out the sounds of the jungle. After a while, the men talked less and less, eventually falling silent, the flashlight no longer searching the walls. Had they decided to wait out the night?

She lay absolutely still, barely daring to breathe. Her limbs were going numb, but she didn't dare move. Passage of time was impossible to judge.

After what she thought might have been a couple of hours, the rain let up. A strange noise was filling the air. The men were talking again. She was pretty sure they were swearing. Had they found something? The odd din grew. Birds. The flapping of wings. But not quite chirping. The alien sound came closer. Something brushed against her leg. Brian cradled her head, his lips close enough to her ear to touch it.

His voice was barely a whisper when he spoke. "Bats."

She jerked against him, but he held her tight. Something swooshed so close she could feel the wind of the wings on her skin. A claw scraped against her scalp.

Her mouth was muffled against Brian's chest before she had a chance to scream.

They were in a bat cave!

And guerillas hunted them below with machine guns.

Things were about as bad as they could get. Then she felt something soft splash on her forehead, and finally figured out what the spongy, rank dirt was below them. They were lying in bat droppings.

She gagged, but pressed her lips together, not daring to make a sound. She buried her face against the chest of the man next to her, who smelled only marginally better than their surroundings, and held on for dear life.

Don't move. The bats won't kill you, but the men below will. Don't panic. She repeated the thought over and over, hypnotizing herself to remain still and silent.

A good hour passed before all the bats were in and settled, and the cave was quiet once again.

"Are the men gone?" she whispered, her nerves as shaky as her limbs.

"They left when the bats started to come home." His chest rose and fell against her cheek. "Damn."

"What?" God, don't let it be more bad news.

"I wanted to get out before the bats got in. If we disturb them now, they'll start swarming and alert everyone around."

"We'll have to stay until they go hunting again?" She didn't have it in her. She couldn't handle it.

"We'll wait a while then see what we can do."

He must have known she was at the end of her rope, because he didn't make her wait long. "Move little by little, a fraction of an inch at a time," he said, and showed her what he meant.

She slid across the slippery rockface in

increments, trying not to think of what she was sliding in. A bat screeched and flapped its wings above. Her heart pounded in her throat, sweat beading on her forehead as she waited.

Brian held still, too. Neither of them dared as much as breathe too hard. The night hunters settled back to sleep above.

More and more light filled the cave now, the sun coming up. Brian tugged on her arm. She kept her gaze on her feet, away from the bats, as she crept after him.

A half an hour passed before they made it off the ledge, but after that the going was easier and faster. Brian signaled her to stay back as he went to check out the cave's entrance.

He limped. She hadn't noticed that last night in the dark. He had seemed to move through the jungle with skill and confidence.

He was gone only a few minutes then stuck his head back in and motioned for her to follow. Thank God, it had been dark when he'd broken her out. He was even scarier in the daylight. If she'd seen him like this she might not have gone with him.

Filthy clothes hung on a surprisingly

muscular body, his hair and beard matted like the fur of a wild animal—with plenty of gray in it. She figured him around fifty. There was a hardness to him, an uncivilized ferocity around his silvery blue eyes that startled her with their intensity. Under any other circumstance, she would have run screaming from the man.

As it was, she followed him deeper into the jungle, brushing bat droppings from her clothes. Who was she to turn up her nose at his appearance? In all likelihood, she didn't look much better.

He moved at a steady pace until they found the creek again. The rain stopped, a small comfort she appreciated. It'd been days since she'd been dry. Her wet clothes chafed her skin with every step she took; her feet felt like they were boiling inside the high-top leather.

He set down the rifle and took off his boots before wading into the water. "You should clean up," he said, fumbling with his mismatched shirt buttons.

"Is it safe?"

"We have a few minutes."

She shook her head and pointed at the creek.

"Fast-moving water is all right. The leeches and the other stuff that'll get you in trouble like stagnant pools. Stand on a stone. Don't drink."

The man didn't have a slow bone in his body. His clothes dropped with much greater speed than she'd been prepared for. He turned from her, but gave no other concession to privacy.

He was all bone and muscle under the dark skin that was a living memorial to the most deprived abuse—a horrifying array of scars visible through the dirt. His hair covered his wide shoulders. He reached for the rag tied around his waist and loosened it.

She looked away.

He probably was used to lack of privacy.

She set her sweaty feet free from the tyranny of the leather boots, and waded downstream. Lord, the cool stream felt good. She bent to wash her hands, then scooped up a handful of water and threw it on her face. If she found a deeper spot somewhere, she could attempt a quick full-body dip. No such luck. A quick scan proved the creek to be evenly shallow.

"Don't go far," Brian called after her. "There are some large predators out there, a bunch of poisonous stuff, too."

He was right. Her guide had been good about pointing out the hazards of the jungle—tigers and snakes on the top of his list. But her brain had been shook up since, her world turned upside down. She relieved herself, watching the bushes, then moved back closer to him.

They were in the middle of the Malaysian jungle, hunted by bloodthirsty guerillas—among other animals. And her sister was— No, she couldn't afford to think about Nicky now—couldn't, or she would fall apart.

She could do this. One step at a time. To save Nicky, she had to keep herself alive. Right now, all she had to focus on was cleaning up. It would help if predators didn't smell her from a mile.

"We can't stay long," he said without turning around. "We're too close to camp."

Audrey pulled her shirt over her head. Undressing in front of a stranger was the least of her worries.

Chapter Two

Brian squeezed the water out of his "underwear," the back piece of an old shirt that had replaced his fallen-apart boxers two years back. He tied the patch of fabric in place before moving on to the rest of his laundry—didn't want the woman to think he was completely uncivilized.

He didn't dare wash his clothes too hard. The pants and shirt were threadbare enough already. The humid air of the jungle was hard on fabric. He sloshed the two pitiful pieces in the clear water and watched for fish, but gave that up after a few minutes. The creek was too shallow and rapid.

Audrey was splashing behind him.

"Try to keep your clothes and body

clean. The smallest injury can get infected in the jungle, even bug bites." He was speaking from experience.

He put his wet pants and shirt back on and sat on a flat rock that got some dappled sunlight from above. There were a few spots over the middle of the creek where the treetops didn't touch.

Then he turned his head and forgot the trees and the sunshine.

Audrey squatted by the edge of the water with her back to him, her wet blond hair streaming past her shoulder blades. She looked like one of the detailed fantasies he had used to pass time with while locked up in the cage. Pearls of water ran down her slim back—creamy skin, delicate curve of the spine—to her round bottom. A groan rumbled up his throat. She might not have looked real, but his body's response certainly was.

He wanted her then and there, on the wet moss—rough and furious. He wanted to empty himself into her. Hot arousal washed through him as he watched her slight movements. He felt his eyes narrow and his nostrils flare, the animal-like need taking him over for a moment, urgent and uncivilized. Then he remembered her face as she had stood by the fire, surrounded by the guerillas.

He got up and strode out of the creek, ashamed that his reaction to her hadn't been any better than theirs. Had they kept him in a cage long enough that he had turned into something that belonged there?

"What are you doing in Malaysia?" He scanned the surrounding trees for food to keep himself busy, and spotted a banana tree. He climbed it while waiting for her response, ignoring the hard-on that made shimmying up the tree more than uncomfortable.

She didn't respond. *Interesting.*

There were plenty of Western tourists in Malaysia, as well as businesspeople. Then there were the crooks who came to the country to make money in the illegal gun trade or drug trafficking. She sure didn't look like she belonged to that group. Of course, appearances could be misleading.

Still, no matter who she was, she didn't

deserve what Omar's men would have done to her.

He reached the top but didn't cut off the whole bunch of bananas. Instead, he broke off enough from here and there for them to eat and tucked them in to his shirt. He didn't want to be slowed down by carrying a load, and he didn't want to leave any telltale signs behind. He cut off a pair of leaves, too, and let them fall to the ground.

Audrey waited for him under the tree with her clothes safely back on, clean but soaking wet, hiding nothing. He wiped his forehead with the back of his hand. Damn, it was hot for this early in the morning.

"I'm on an adoption trip with my sister," she said, folding her arms in front of her.

From the way her moss-green eyes glistened as she spoke, he figured the sister wasn't back at the Kuala Lumpur Grand Hotel, soaking in a hot tub. Since she wasn't here with Audrey, it was safe to assume she'd been killed when the guerillas had attacked them.

Unsure what to say, he offered her a banana and slung Ahmad's AK-47 over his shoulder. It had to be hard to lose a sibling. He could only imagine the special closeness between two people who shared the same blood. He'd never had that with anyone.

"I was adopted," he said.

She looked up from peeling, her eyes luminous in the sunshine.

Damn. Where the hell had that come from? It wasn't something he shared. He looked down, embarrassed at having said something so personal.

His gaze settled on her footwear. And seeing a problem he could fix, the next second he was back in professional soldier mode again. "Give me your boots."

She only hesitated a second before she sat to unlace them. When she handed him the first, he shoved his knife inside and made a couple of small holes in the leather, close to the sole, then repeated the procedure with the other one.

"What's that for?"

"So that moisture can get out. Whether we make it or not will depend on how fast and how far we can walk. Always take care of your feet."

She nodded and put the boots back on.

He picked up a banana leaf, cut and twisted it until it resembled a very primitive wide-brimmed hat, then put it on her head. "It'll keep the creepy crawlers from falling into your shirt neck from above," he said, and made one for himself.

"I used to have a hat. It fell off in the boat. Thank you."

So she had come up the river. He'd pretty much figured that. Boat travel was the easiest way to get around in these parts. Which was exactly why he couldn't steal a canoe and paddle out. The river would be the first place where Omar's men would look for them, and there would be no place to hide on the water. As hard as it was going to be, they had no choice but to walk out. And they better get to it. "Come on. We'll eat as we go."

She fell in step behind him as he moved forward, listening for anything unusual in the cacophony of birdcalls. He could make out the sound of a couple of monkeys arguing in the distance, but nothing suspicious caught his attention.

"Are we going to a village?"

"To the river." Most villages in the vicinity were controlled by the guerillas. "It's called the Baram."

The night before, he had run off to the opposite direction, knowing he couldn't cross it in the dark with the woman in tow. "We have to circle back to it, get over to the other side and follow it to Miri."

"Can't we cross later? Shouldn't we be moving away from the guerillas?"

She was thinking and not following him blindly. Good. It showed presence of mind. They were going to need that. "We'll come out above the camp. They'll be watching the river below. That's the way out. The sooner we cross, the better. The farther down we get, the wider the Baram becomes."

She accepted that without argument. He liked that, too. She was independent enough to think for herself if needed, but smart enough to accept his authority. The strength of the team they forged would play a big part in their survival. So far, she was okay.

A fine mist started to drizzle from above,

nothing that would slow them down, just enough to get them wet. There were more caves ahead, a good ten miles from here. If they reached them by noon, they could rest there, maybe light a fire to dry their clothes.

She finished eating and held out the peel. "What do I do with this?"

She knew now not to leave a trail. He grunted in approval as he took the peel from her, then handed her another banana. Maybe they stood a slim chance of making it out of here after all. He felt a twinge of guilt at having had considered leaving her behind with Omar. She hadn't turned out as bad as he had expected. But she would have to get better still.

When the last piece of fruit was gone, he stopped and buried their leavings, then held out the AK-47. "You know how to use this?"

She shook her head.

"Not much to it. Just aim and squeeze the trigger." He waited until she took the gun, tested its weight, held it to her shoulder. She looked unsure of herself, but at least she was giving it a try. He nodded to her with encouragement when she handed the rifle back, then turned and continued walking. "In case something happens to me," he said, "keep east by the sun."

Better to be prepared for every eventuality.

He had learned that lesson well as a marine, then again when he'd entered special training after being recruited into the SDDU, Special Designation Defense Unit, America's secret weapon against terrorism. SDDU soldiers were expected to be the best of the best, and damn, it had stroked his ego to have been chosen. They had better weapons and more freedom to use them than anyone, and didn't have to report to Congress or any military chain of command, but went straight to the Homeland Security Secretary.

Hell, Congress and all those generals didn't even know the SDDU existed. The unit had been created to deal with problems that couldn't be addressed in the open. To effectively fight terrorists who broke every rule, the U.S. needed a team that didn't have any rules tying their hands, either. And that was the SDDU.

It really burned him that he had gotten taken out on his first mission. And the fact that he would never now pass the physical to get back in got under his skin even more.

"Keep your eyes and ears open. If we come across trouble, drop and roll to cover."

Brian pushed forward, ignoring the pain in his bad leg. The old injury made a big difference. Not just the limp, but how weak the muscles were. It had been a while since he'd walked any farther than the bushes to relieve himself.

He had exercised over the years with the guerillas, done more push-ups and sit-ups than any ten men in a lifetime, but it was hard to exercise his legs in a cage that didn't allow him to stand up. He hated the weakness, the knowledge that he was outnumbered and outgunned. And if that wasn't bad enough, he had the woman depending on him now, raising the stakes of failure.

Damn. Things hadn't exactly turned out as he had expected. She ended up being more capable than he had thought, and he less so. It ticked him off and so did the sudden doubts that assailed him. Had he done the right thing by dragging her into the jungle? He had thought he could protect her, but what if he couldn't?

What the hell made him think she was better off with him? Maybe Omar would have reined in his men. Her letter would be on its way to her family by now. Sure as hell, he could offer her no guarantees.

"Thank you for bringing me with you," she said from behind at the exact worst moment.

He turned back to her. Didn't she realize they were in just as much danger now, if not more, than in the guerilla camp?

"You can thank me later. If we make it out of the jungle alive."

HAMID WENT THROUGH the plans, thinking of the men he had chosen, reevaluating them one by one. He trusted them as much as he trusted anyone. The first phase of his plan looked good to go, but phase two bothered him.

His men had taken too many hostages. Americans, too, which could spell trouble. Westerners didn't understand this part of the world, weren't willing to play by its rules. He had made a fortune and financed a veritable army by picking up a Japanese or Russian businessman now and then, demanding silence and ransom from their families.

This time, it might be different. Just the scale of the kidnapping guaranteed that the government and media would get wind of it. He hoped to hell they didn't choose to interfere. A smooth transaction was in everyone's best interest.

He shuffled the papers and cursed Muhammad, the captain responsible for this mess. Muhammad was greedy, both for money and power. He bore watching.

The steel door opened and one of his men came in. "A messenger came from Omar."

From Omar. It had happened then. He nodded his approval to let the messenger in, only slightly surprised, with a faint regret for the death of Jamil, who had been a friend in the old days. So the younger brother took the camp. It wasn't altogether unexpected.

Omar was another man he wouldn't want to turn his back to. In fact, Muhammad reminded him of Omar a lot.

The messenger looked unsure of himself as he conveyed his leader's greetings.

Hamid waved away the formalities. "How are things with my friend, Omar?"

"Jamil had an accident."

He expressed his regrets, having no illusions about what had happened. Most likely, the *accident* had been a bullet in the back. Omar had been coveting his brother's position for years.

Hamid leaned back in his chair, considering how this would effect his plans. He had been trying to get Jamil to join the operation, but Jamil had dragged his heels, disliking making war on civilians. Omar had no compunctions, which would make things easier. But could a man who would kill his own blood be trusted?

He watched the messenger closely. "All is well in camp?"

The man looked down. "We had a hostage that escaped."

Hamid lifted an eyebrow. Omar wasted no time going after money, did he? "The jungle will take care of him." He shrugged.

"It was a woman. That soldier prisoner broke out and took her with him."

He sat up straight, interested now, knowing well of Jamil's foreign soldier, the man he had insisted on keeping against advice. It was a running joke in the camps, how Jamil got stuck with him, wanting to make a point to his younger brother on who made the decisions.

That man could make it out of the jungle. That man could bring the army back with him. "When?"

"Yesterday."

"Omar has everyone out looking?"

The messenger nodded, looking more nervous now than when he had arrived.

"Did anything else happen?"

"He—the prisoner—got some notes Omar sent you about Jamil...."

"And?"

"He pledged his help with the attacks."

He stood up so fast he knocked the chair over. Swore. Damn the incompetent son of a bitch. He would not have his operation compromised now, not when everything was ready to go.

"Anything that would give us away?"

"That's all he told me," the man rushed to say.

He called out, and two fighters rushed in.

"Jamil's prisoner escaped yesterday. Send as many men as you can. Have Muhammad take them." This once, his captain was welcome to go overboard.

COME ON. COME BACK.

Audrey sat by the cave's entrance, the AK-47 laid across her legs as she stared into the jungle. She had no idea what time it was. Her watch, along with her jewelry, was the first thing the guerillas had taken after they had captured her.

Brian hadn't been gone more than a half hour, an hour at tops, but it felt like ten. She had plenty of time to worry about a whole list of worst-case scenarios. Like what would she do if a tiger decided to pay her a visit, or the guerillas found her, or something happened to Brian and he didn't come back.

She rubbed her eyes. God, she was driving herself nuts. Brian would be back soon. Everything was going to be fine.

He had gone off to see if he could scare up some meat. They needed protein for strength, couldn't survive on fruit, he'd said. He'd promised to build a fire when he came back. She decided to focus on that. Her clothes were no longer soaking wet, but still damp enough to be uncomfortable.

He would be back for her. She had to believe that. She listened to the birdcalls above, watched for the burst of color that flashed between the branches now and then.

Was Nicky out there somewhere looking up at the trees, same as her? Dear God, let her be unharmed.

Something rustled in the undergrowth to the left. Her muscles tensed, her heart in her throat in an instant. She tried to see beyond the profusion of green fronds, but couldn't make out anything. She gripped the gun and drew farther back into the cave.

More noise, then a branch snapping. She held her breath. Brian? She didn't dare call out. Then she saw the fronds move. Something was definitely there, coming toward her.

A young fighter stepped into the clearing, scanning the area, rifle at the ready.

Her blood raced so fast it made her dizzy. She held her breath, hoping he couldn't see her in the darkness of the cave.

But he did, and smiled when their eyes met.

He called back, a single word, but no response came from behind him, which gave her hope. Maybe he had wandered out of hearing distance from the others.

She scampered back toward the deeper reaches of the cave, gripping her own gun in her sweaty palms, although she didn't dare shoot. She had never shot anything. Her chances of hitting him were one in a million.

If she started shooting he would shoot back, with considerably more skill than she had. And a gunshot, too, could alert the rest of his group to their whereabouts. She would only use the rifle if she had no other choice, and only if she was sure she would hit him.

As young as he was, she was no match for him. Escape and evade, the term she'd heard Brian use popped into her head. Panic propelled her forward as she turned to run, seeing less and less the farther in she got. Her boots slammed against stone, the sound echoing in the cave, mixing with the slap of her pursuer's steps.

Brian had said there were lime caves in these mountains that went on for miles underground. If this one had a fraction of that space— If she could evade this man until Brian came back— She rushed into a dark corridor, gasped the musty air, fear sending her lungs into overdrive.

Blindly she ran forward, her hands stretched in front of her in the darkness, hoping the path was straight. It wasn't. She smacked into the stone wall and dropped the gun, bent to search for it but felt nothing other than small rocks, cold and sharp under her fingertips. It had to be here. She swept the ground, frantic.

The man was close enough for her to hear his breathing, smell his sweat. Forget the gun. Her hand on the wall, she moved ahead, hoping for a fork in the road, or a crevice she could flatten herself into while he went by.

She hadn't walked a few steps when she was brought hard to the ground. The pain in the side of her skull was blinding. Her head spun for a moment as she struggled against the weight that pinned her down. She clawed at him, felt his fingers close around one wrist first, then the other as he swore in the darkness.

"No. Please." She tried to catch her breath.

He pulled her to her feet and dragged her toward the light. She kicked and missed. He shook her and dragged her on, threw her to the ground once they were back in the larger cavern that received enough sunlight to see.

He asked something she couldn't understand. She shook her head as she sat up, then noticed the knife in his belt and lunged for it.

He outmaneuvered her with ease, but ended up falling on her, pressing her back into the sharp rocks.

Shouldn't have done that. Shouldn't have gone for his weapon. She had really pissed him off. The sight of his anger-reddened face paralyzed her limbs. Then his features changed as he brought up a hand to cup her breast.

"Stop." She struggled against him with new desperation.

He reached between them and ripped her pants. A scream pushed its way up her throat but she swallowed it back. His people were probably closer than Brian. She didn't want them to find her. There was a slim chance she might be able to fight off this one, but if the rest came, she was finished.

She felt around with shaking hands for a suitable rock on the ground. Nothing but dirt and gravel. Figured. At least a half-dozen rocks dug against her ribs. She tried to twist aside, but the man on top of her wouldn't allow her the movement.

Expect the worse. Expect that you're going to get hurt. The words of some self-defense expert from a TV show a couple of years ago floated back to her. She had to keep a clear head, resist the panic, look for an opportunity.

The man on top of her was stronger than she, and it wasn't even so much his extra bulk of muscles, but that he knew how to fight. She could do nothing to stop him.

Accepting the inevitable brought a strange sense of control. When he violated her body, there would be a moment of advantage. She would wait for that moment and try again for his knife. She would not allow him to take her back to camp. That was the most important thing. No matter what else he did, he must not keep her from her mission. Not when her sister's life depended on her.

She steeled herself, but instead of the pain she expected, the man's head snapped back and he fell from her. Brian slit the attacker's throat with one smooth move from ear to ear and shoved the lifeless body to the side.

"Are you all right?" He turned to her.

She stared at the gushing blood and threw up the bananas.

When Brian stepped forward, she backed away in horror. He towered over her, his hands bloody. *It was okay. He was okay.* He was the guy who had saved her, she told herself, but her brain had trouble catching up.

He stood for a moment, looking at her, then went to squat next to the man and search the body. She looked away, gagging anew at the sight of the blood that was now pooling on the ground.

"We have to get moving," he said a minute later.

She nodded and stood, held her pants together with one hand as she walked toward the opening of the cave.

"Where is the other gun?" Brian left the man and was coming toward her with the new rifle and the extra knife.

She flinched away. "Back in the corridor. I dropped it." Her voice trembled. "It's too dark to see in there."

He looked her over, then went back to the fallen man, took his belt and held it out for her. She couldn't bring herself to touch it. Brian nodded and gave her the rope that held up his own pants. When she didn't move, he helped her tie her khakis in place, touching her as little as possible. She was shaking by the time he was done.

"There are a half-dozen guerillas a quarter mile downhill. Stay behind me and stay quiet," he said as he stepped out of the cave.

Chapter Three

His knee was killing him. Brian looked up, but could not see the sun from the thick canopy above. Still, it had to be close to the end of the day. The animals were beginning to make their evening sounds, and light had dimmed a little in the last half hour or so. Night fell fast in the jungle, and they hadn't found shelter yet. The hillside was supposed to be riddled with caves. Just not when you were looking for one.

"We'll stop here," he said.

At least the rain had quit for now. He leaned his gun against a tree trunk and scanned the ground for some dry leaves and twigs. But, of course, everything was wet and so were they. The air was cooling off fast. Their soaked-through clothing would be cold and uncomfortable during the night, if he didn't manage to make a fire.

He was used to this state of miserable affairs, but she wasn't. If she got sick and weak it would slow them down, and that was something they couldn't afford. And there was the matter of food, too. While he would have been fine with eating the meat raw, he doubted she felt the same. "Look for anything you think might burn."

"Won't a fire give us away?"

"Nobody walks in the jungle at night unless they absolutely have to. The chance of injury is too high, too easy to fall into something, getting bitten by things you can't see." He didn't mention the night predators, didn't want to make her too nervous to sleep. "My guess is Omar and his band will hole up somewhere for the night and start out fresh in the morning, hoping they'll come across our trail."

He reached for the paper in his shirt pocket. Soaking wet. Figured. A few minutes passed before he found a handful of dry leaves under a bush. He crumbled the leaves into a small pile, set a chunk of dry bark on top of them. From his shirt, he got some of the rope Audrey had been tied up with. That was wet, too, but it didn't matter for his purposes. He peeled off a quarter-inch strand and made a small bow with a green stick. Then he found a dry one, sharpened one end and placed it in the middle of the bark next to the tinder and began moving it with the bow, as fast as he could, putting on the pressure.

He saw Audrey shiver from the corner of his eye. It would have been good if he could have brought the shirt from the man he'd taken out at the cave, but he had to leave it behind. The last thing you wanted in the jungle was to smell like blood. She probably wouldn't have put it on anyway.

"Can I do anything?"

"No," he said at first, then changed his mind and instructed her on how to make a sleeping platform. Better for both of them if she pulled her own weight. If anything happened to him, her life would be easier if she'd learned a few skills. He worked on

making the fire while he explained what
needed to be done.

An hour went by, maybe two, before he
caught the faint scent of smoke—he had lost
his once keen sense of time while in the
cage. He blew gently on the leaves until he
saw the first ember glow in the night that had
fallen around them. He gave it more air then
fed the small fire. There. They would be fine.

Audrey brought him a handful of dry
twigs.

He took the wood with a nod. "Are you
all right?"

She hadn't said a word since they had
left the cave. He had let her be, not wanting to push.

"Fine."

The fire had grown enough so he could
see her face now. Her expression was som-
ber, but the shock and revulsion he'd seen
at the cave were gone. She had been scared
out of her wits. The man he had been four
years ago could have comforted her. Now
he had no idea what to say, what to do.

He was no good for her. Hell, he was
probably no good for anyone. For anything.

The question he had tried to avoid wouldn't go away. How was he supposed to go back to normal civilian life?

Because he definitely couldn't go back to his job at the SDDU. Not with his bad leg. That position was history. Trouble was, he didn't know how to do anything else.

For a moment back in the cave, she had looked at him as if he was as much of a monster as the man he had pulled off her. She was probably right. But by God, he wanted it to be different.

"I had to do that," he said quietly. "You're safe with me."

"I know." She lifted her gaze to him. "I should have handled it better. You did it for my sake."

Her acceptance loosened some of the tight darkness inside him. The light of the flames bathed her face in a warm glow as she looked straight into his eyes without a trace of fear or loathing.

"I was trying to reach his knife. I think if I did, I might have done the same."

"Sometimes you don't have a choice."

She nodded. "You saved my life twice. Thank you."

She reached out and put a hand on his, briefly, warm and soft. He jerked away on reflex, not used to human touch that didn't hurt, then swore as he burned the back of his wrist in the fire.

Startled, she pulled away.

Damn. "Which one of you was going to adopt?" he asked—the first question that came to his mind.

"Me."

He took a slow breath as he untied the small bundle that hung from his shoulder. "How come your husband didn't come with you?"

"I don't have a husband."

He opened the sack he'd woven from strips of palm leaves to carry the squirrel-like animal he had killed earlier.

"One of those independent women?"

"One of those women whose husband couldn't take the stress of infertility treatments and left her for a simpler relationship," she said quietly.

"Sounds like a real jerk." She was still

young, though. He figured her for thirty, if that, with all kinds of possibilities still ahead of her.

She didn't respond.

"Sorry. It's none of my business."

"It's okay. And Josh is okay, too. I mean—I guess, some things just aren't meant to be." Sadness laced her voice.

Why the hell had he brought up this topic? Damn, he sucked at the pep-talk thing. Better focus on something he knew how to do.

He skewered their dinner—had already skinned and gutted the squirrel when he caught it—and held their meal above the flames. There was pitifully little meat on the bones, hardly enough for one person, let alone two, but it was better than nothing. They would manage.

She combed her fingers through her damp hair and moved closer to the fire. "How long have you been here?"

"Four years." The words burned his throat.

She looked up at him wide-eyed. "Have you ever tried to escape before?"

Hell, yes. That's how he had known about the caves. But they had caught him each time. He had been too impatient, trying to make a break for it before he had his strength back.

He shrugged. "For the first year, I couldn't walk. Then I got malaria and was too weak to get away. I did try, mind you. Then they stuck me in a damn cage."

"Why didn't they ransom you?"

"They didn't know who to ask for money. I wouldn't tell them who I was. And they thought I might have some useful information."

Then by the time they figured out he wouldn't talk, the disagreement over his fate had been too public of a quarrel. Jamil couldn't shoot him at that point without making it seem like he was bending to his younger brother's will. And they couldn't let him go, either. He had seen too much. Sometimes he wondered if Jamil was simply waiting for him to give up the fight and die.

Audrey was looking at him in bewilderment. "Why would they think you had any information that concerned them?"

"It's a long story."

"Are you some kind of a spy or something?" she asked after a while, staring at him with suspicion.

"Military."

"Why didn't they come to rescue you?"

"They don't know I'm alive."

His team had been spread out in the jungle, looking for a group of Muslim extremists who had crossed the border from Indonesia to purchase explosives. He had found a cache of TNT in an underground bunker, called in the location. Unfortunately, the Malaysian military had chosen that day to crack down on some bothersome guerillas and had dropped a couple of bombs over the forest where they'd thought the guerillas had been hiding. One of the bombs had hit the bunker.

The force of the explosion had thrown him clear, which was the only reason he had survived—with his skin torn off his side, his leg broken in several places and a severe concussion. Jamil and his men had found him, taken him with them. He remembered little of those first weeks.

They'd recognized him as a soldier and had questioned him when he'd recovered. When he wouldn't speak, Omar had re-broken his leg.

"Do you have a family back in Montana?"

He turned the meat over the fire. "My parents have passed away. They adopted me when they were older." And marriage had never been in the cards for him. It didn't mesh with his job. "Do you have any other siblings?"

"Just Nicky."

"It must have been hard losing her."

A look of determination crossed her face. "I'm going to find her and get her back."

"She's alive? Why didn't Omar's men bring her back to camp?"

"A little over a week ago, we were supposed to go on a four-day tour to Gunung Mulu National Park. I had to stay behind at the last minute. The judge was asking for more documentation for the adoption and I was meeting with the lawyer I hired here, so Nicky went alone. Not alone, I mean. A whole group went with a guide." She looked down at her hands. "They were attacked by guerillas and twelve tourists were taken hostage. The demand is a million dollars per person."

She had to be kidding. "You came to the jungle to rescue her?"

"I came to pay the ransom." She reached under her shirt and pulled out a crumpled, wet piece of paper. "It's a bank account I opened a couple of days ago."

He glanced at the smudged printout that showed a cool million as account total.

"The Malaysian government is negotiating with the guerillas and told the family members to stay put, but I couldn't do it. These things never end well. The military will attack, half the hostages won't make it. I've seen it on TV before…. No government will ever admit that they don't have everything under control."

"So you grabbed a million from your savings and ran off into the jungle? How were you planning on finding them? Does the government know where they are?"

She shook her head. "They're still gathering intelligence. My brother-in-law wired the money."

"Why isn't he here?"

"He's coming. I just— I didn't want to wait. I hired a local guide who said he could take me to a village frequented by the guerillas."

"There are dozens of guerilla groups scattered over the island."

"I figured they could point me in the right direction."

"And what were you going to do when you got to the ones who have your sister?"

"Show them the account to prove that the money is here in the country, have one of the men come with me and Nicky to the nearest bank. I would have had the money wired there and given him the cash. He walks out with the money, I walk out with Nicky."

All right, there was a slim chance it could have worked, if she made it as far as the right guerilla camp, but trusting her fate to the first group of bandits she had come across had been a mistake. "There's no honor among thieves."

She gave him a don't-I-know-it look. "The guide led me to a village high up the hills and disappeared by morning. Then the fighters came and took me with them. They had me bound and gagged, I couldn't even talk to them."

"I used to have some connections," he said, surprising himself. "When we get to the nearest town, Miri, I'll see what I can do about your sister." He had a pretty good idea where the hostages were.

"How far is Miri?"

"A good week of walking if we don't run into any trouble."

He saw her pale in the firelight.

"I don't have a week. The ransom deadline is in four days."

Damn. He clamped his jaw together, fighting the inevitable.

She pulled her knees up and wrapped her arms around them, her eyes wide with desperation. "What if I allowed myself to be recaptured? I could show the fighters the bank statement and tell them they would get a reward if they took me to the group who has the hostages. Maybe you could follow us to make sure nothing bad happened," she added, barely disguised hope all over her heart-shaped face.

"That's not how it works, Audrey. These people don't engage in dialogue." He wanted to make her understand. "It would be like it was back at the cave."

She went still and after a moment, nodded.

"They might shoot you on sight because you made them chase you around. Or they might do worse. And if you told them about the money, they would take you to the bank to get it without going anywhere near your sister."

She stayed silent for a while. "You're right," she said, her eyes glistening. "I failed."

He hated the misery on her face. She'd come here to adopt a child, and her sister had come to help. It wasn't fair.

Then again, what in life was?

He watched her struggle with her tears and something twisted inside him, an emotion he barely recognized shook loose—compassion. He opened his mouth. This was a bad idea. He drew in a lungful of jungle air, a mixture of the musty smell of decomposing leaves and the light scent of orchids. "We'll get your sister back."

In an instant, her eyes filled with so much hope and trust, he had to look away. Sure as hell, he didn't deserve anyone looking at him that way.

He had to be insane. The captivity had done it to him, and the beatings. Somewhere along the line he had lost his mind. Because if he wasn't one hundred percent stir-crazy, he wouldn't have committed himself to overtaking a guerilla camp alone.

No, not alone. Alone would have been a step up from what he was planning to do. He was going to try to pull off a major operation with a civilian in tow.

FINE, MISTY RAIN dampened her hair, but had not yet soaked her clothes.

"You know, the travel agent was right. She said Malaysia had two seasons, wet and very wet." Audrey licked her fingers, still hungry, but at least not starving. Their dinner had been reduced to a tiny pile of bones next to the dying fire.

She was about to fall over with exhaustion. The last time she'd slept she'd barely gotten a few fitful minutes on the bottom of the boat, gagged and bound, on her way to the guerilla camp. The desperation she had felt then slammed back into her anew. She couldn't shake a sense of dread, a premonition that getting Nicky back would be far more difficult than she had first imagined.

"Give me your pants."

Excuse me? She looked at Brian across the fire.

He picked up a thighbone from the pile, put it on a rock and smashed it with a smaller chunk of stone. "I'm gonna fix the rip." He chose a long, thin sliver of bone and worked it with his knife, drilling a hole in one end.

A needle. She stood and tugged at the rope. Having to use it to hold up her pants had been a pain. If she tied it loose, her clothes kept escaping; if she tied it tight, it cut into her abdomen. She fumbled. The fibers had swollen from moisture.

"Hang on."

He came around the fire to help and got

on his knees in front of her, his dreadlocks sticking out in every which direction. She sucked in her stomach to give him room to work.

The wildman of the jungle was helping her take off her clothes. Her life had crossed over from the insane to the bizarre.

The rope loosened, and he returned to his spot without looking at her. He seemed to know instinctually what she needed and when—food, protection, privacy—and gave it without thought. She sat back down, took off her boots and pulled the bottom of her pants from her socks where they'd been secured to keep the bugs out.

"Here we go." He peeled a thin string from the rope and licked the end to smooth down the fibers.

She took off the pants and tucked her shirt around her legs. It came to midthigh. She glanced at Brian across the fire. "Hopefully, the bugs won't do too much damage. They can't eat me in just a few minutes, right?"

His hands shook as he tried to thread the needle, the movement slight at first, then growing more pronounced. The muscles in his face tightened with each attempt. She had noticed the shaking before, a trembling that came to his fingers and passed after a while. His nerves were shot. That he'd survived at all was in itself a miracle.

"Let me do that." She held out her hand.

He hesitated for a moment, his eyes burning like silver flames of an unearthly fire, then dropped the needle and thread into her palm. She wanted to say something to lighten his mood, but what did you say to comfort a man whose life had been stolen away? What could she possibly say that would make the past four years okay? She focused on the needle and went to work.

He didn't stay idle, either. When she glanced up, he was rubbing two chunks of hard sandstone against each other. He didn't stop until he got a flat surface on one. He waited until the mist wet it, picked up the smaller of his two knives and worked the blade over the rock with smooth movements, away from him, clockwise first then anti-clockwise. The sound sent shivers down her spine, reminding her of old horror movies.

Maybe it was the darkness that seemed to have swallowed them that turned her thoughts so morbid. The night was a solid black wall starting a few feet from their campfire, surrounding them. The calls of wild animals, like that of angry invisible ghosts, startled her from time to time, made her draw closer to the flames.

She had been able to appreciate the beauty of the jungle when she had first seen it on the peninsula shortly after their arrival. It had seemed a living, breathing marvel. Now she found it threatening.

Brian examined the knife at the light of the flames, then took his shirt off. As scary as his appearance was in general, his body was beautiful, despite the scars. And she appreciated the strength in it that had saved her life.

He grabbed his beard with his left hand and began to hack away with the right, tufts of hair falling at his feet. Once he was down to the last inch or so, he gathered some water from the palm leaves next to him, wet the stubble thoroughly, then shaved.

She put down the needle, grabbed the larger knife from the ground and cut off the extra thread, then put her pants and boots back on. There was nothing else to do but watch his progress. His hands had steadied. And thank God for that. She wasn't sure she would have been brave enough to offer her help with shaving, not with that deadly looking blade.

The fire was down to embers when he moved on to his hair. There hadn't been enough dry material to keep the flames going, but whatever they'd managed was enough. They had a hot meal in their stomachs and were warmed up a little. If nothing else, it lifted her spirits, which was probably one of the most important things. If she could keep her mind from sinking into despair and giving up, the battle would be half-won.

Brian cut the hair on the side methodically and progressed to the back, his movements turning awkward.

"Let me help." She rose and went to him. "Turn around."

She knelt behind him and worked fast,

cutting as much by feel as sight. He tossed what had remained of the ropes that had once bound her into the fire, but the fibers were damp and gave but a few more minutes of light, producing plenty of smoke in the process. Then the last ember blinked out and they were shrouded in darkness.

"Here's the knife." She held it out to where she'd last seen his hand.

"You keep it," he said.

She tightened her fingers on the handle, unsure where to put the small weapon.

He didn't move.

What was he waiting for?

She should probably brush the hair off his back. She shifted, reluctant to touch him. And how stupid was that? He had saved her life twice, had just given her a knife that was sharp enough to shave with. He wasn't about to throw her to the ground, for heaven's sake. She reached out with her left hand and brushed the clippings off, quick, businesslike. It was strange to touch him like this, feeling without seeing, the long ridges of his scars pressing against her fingertips. For someone as underfed as he was, he retained an amazing amount of muscle.

She snatched away her hand and stood in one motion, stepping back.

"Thank you," he said, his voice deep and thick.

She could hear him put on his shirt and move over to the raised platform she had built while he'd started their short-lived fire. He had instructed her on how to make a frame, how to stack on top the two dozen or so fallen branches he'd asked her to gather. She hoped the vines would hold and they wouldn't tumble to the ground in the middle of the night, although, they weren't high up—no more than a foot or so—just enough to keep the bugs and rats and snakes off them.

She stepped after him and felt for the edge of the platform, big enough for the two of them to sleep on without touching.

"Good haircut," he said, "by the feel of it."

"I wasn't taking a big risk. Anything had to be an improvement."

"It was that bad, huh?" There was a rare lightness to his voice.

"Scary."

"You don't strike me as the type who scares easily."

Shows what you know. She was scared of the jungle. She was scared for Nicky. She was even a little scared of him. First time in bed with a wildman, and all.

"What do you do at home when you're not dashing off to rescue people?"

"I work at a drug and alcohol rehab clinic." She had resigned her director of admissions position just before leaving for Malaysia, and took a cut in pay and title so she'd have more time to spend with her baby when they got back. And she was scared about that, too. If, after all the dreaming and hoping, she wouldn't turn out to be a good mother.

"So the urge to rescue runs deep in the blood."

Was he teasing her? The deadpan comment seemed so out of character, she was unsure how to respond.

"I had a boyfriend in high school who died of a drug overdose. I didn't even know he was using. He was class valedictorian.

I got involved in every antidrug support program after that. Things just progressed from there, I suppose."

She fidgeted on the bed.

"Know of a good twelve-step program for recovering washed-out POWs?" His voice was hard again, not a trace of lightness left in it.

She wanted desperately to say something that would help him, something that went beyond the usual you're-in-control-of-your-future platitude. In a sense, he was similar to the men and women she dealt with at work every day. Their lives were robbed from them by the substances they abused, just as the guerillas had stolen years from Brian. And yet in many other ways, he was profoundly different.

"Good night," he said, closing the conversation before she could form a response.

She was up long after his breathing evened, startled by a call or shriek of some wild animal every time she began to doze off. Small noises came from above, insects and God knows what else dropping on the palm leaf roof Brian had thrown together after he had coaxed the fire to life.

Her mind was restless, going to Nicky over and over again, wondering how she was doing, if her sister was still alive. Her clothes were damp and she was cold, wishing back the cave where they'd spent the previous night. Amazing what a difference dry clothes made.

Brian mumbled something.

"What?"

He spoke again, in another language. She could hear him kicking at the leaves that she'd piled onto the bamboo platform for comfort. Maybe he was having a nightmare. He probably had enough bad memories to fill a lifetime of scary dreams. She had only spent a day with the guerillas. He had been their prisoner for four years. She couldn't begin to comprehend what he had gone through.

The thought brought a slew of uncomfortable questions. What right did she have to ask him to go back? He had already suffered more than most people she knew did in a lifetime. He needed rest and sufficient food, and medical care for his bad leg.

She was prepared to risk everything to save her sister, even her life. But she had no right to ask him to do the same.

He kicked again, wildly, and must have hit one of the supports because the shelter rattled. She reached out and her fingers brushed against his face, registering how cold his wet skin was a split second before his hand closed around her wrist—tight enough to hurt.

Fear slammed into her. They couldn't see each other. He could snap her neck before he woke enough to remember her. "Brian?" She scrambled away from him as far as she could.

He eased his grip and a second later let her go.

"Sorry," he said after a while, his voice raspy from sleep.

"You had a bad dream." She rubbed her wrist, staying back.

Silence followed her words.

"Look," she said after a few minutes. "You don't have to come with me. If you could just take me close enough so I can get to them without getting lost." That would be enough. She would show the bank statement, and after that things should resolve quickly.

"I wouldn't hurt you," he said over his shoulder, misunderstanding her. "I said you could trust me."

"It's not that I don't. I do. But don't you think you've had enough? I'm grateful that you saved my life. But it's not your job to watch over me. You don't owe me anything." She said the words awfully bravely, even though she didn't feel very brave at the moment.

"We'll get your sister."

She wanted to protest and pretend that she wasn't melting in relief, but she couldn't bring herself to do it. She did need him, want him with her. He was offering. She wasn't stupid enough to fight him on this.

A steady drizzle came from above, some of it dripping through the makeshift roof. She pulled in her neck and wrapped her arms around herself. Under her brand-new shirt, she had on a cotton T-shirt and a thin cotton tanktop with a built-in bra under that—three layers of clothing and she was still shivering. Brian's shirt was torn in a couple of places, worn thin with use.

She scooted closer to him until she was touching his back.

He pulled away.

Chapter Four

Brian stared into the forest that glistened in the rising dawn, and planned their route. They'd cross the Baram and go upriver on land instead of on the water. He didn't want to run into anyone who used the river. Omar wouldn't be looking for them in that direction, but he didn't want to be seen by anyone at all. News of strangers in the jungle had a way of spreading.

At least they didn't have to worry about food—fruit shouldn't be hard to find this time of the year. And he could hunt, too, although only if they came across easy prey—he couldn't afford to waste time.

He listened as unseen animals called to each other in the distance. The jungle didn't scare him. It was merely an obstacle they had to overcome.

Audrey's warm body pressed against his back—drawing him into a territory a hell of a lot more dangerous than the wild forest.

Her proximity was comforting and arousing at the same time. She'd rolled against him in her sleep at one point during the night, and he hadn't been able to find the strength to move away again.

The first substantial nonmalicious human contact he'd had in years. It left him weak in the knees. Damn, he was a sap. Pitiful. He had spent the night fighting the urge to turn to her, unable to sleep since she'd woken him.

He didn't know what he wanted from her—not all of him, anyway. His body had no doubts, but he tried to force his mind to run along more civilized lines. He wasn't sure what was right, what was realistic.

She was his responsibility, but she was all his fantasies come true, too. And she had earned his respect in the past twenty-four hours they'd spent together.

She was loyal, ready to give her life for

family and brave, if a little misguided. Coming to look for the guerillas had been a less than well-thought-out plan, but he could understand her desperation.

He felt her stir then pull away, and rolled onto his back. He got lost looking at her mussed hair and sleep-heavy eyes.

"What?"

"You look beautiful." He hadn't meant to say that. The words came out choppy, like a rusty reflex. It had been a while since he'd last paid a compliment to a woman.

A rueful smile tugged up her tempting lips. "Thanks. But I'm going to have to take into consideration that you haven't been surrounded by women lately." She hesitated for a moment, then added, "You're not half as scary without the beard."

That was a start. She was obviously warming up to him. It was the first attempt she'd made at a joke since they'd met.

"We better get going before the rain starts again." He slid off the platform and stood, for a second just enjoying the luxury of being able to stand tall whenever he wanted.

Something else was standing tall, too. Just a morning thing. She didn't control his body. Right.

"We'll get breakfast where we find it. You can go to the bathroom over there." He nodded to a wide-trunked palm to his left. "I'll be behind those trees. Keep your knife handy."

He picked up her semidry socks and boots and handed them to her, then got his own.

When they were both back, he bent a large, slightly cone-shaped leaf that was filled with rainwater, so she could wash her hands and face, and another so she could drink.

She had a slim, long neck—plenty of landing space for a platoon of kisses. He watched her swallow until he was getting hot and bothered again and decided it was best not to look.

After she was done and he had his fill as well, he broke off the leaf, dried it on his pants and folded it into a pouch. He collected his hair from the ground and packed it in, tying the leaf-bag to his belt with a piece of vine when he was done. "Tinder," he said before making another pouch and filling that one with ashes. He looped the rope around his shoulder, tucked away the needle. They started out as soon as he was done.

"Shouldn't we cover up all this?" She glanced back toward their makeshift camp.

He liked it that she was always thinking. It had been a long time since anyone had his back.

"We're far enough now. We shouldn't have to worry about Omar's men." Not that they were safe from the guerillas altogether. Different groups controlled the various areas of the mountain. But enough of the locals from the villages came into the jungle for hunting trips so that leftovers of a small camp wouldn't raise any suspicions if a couple of fighters came across it.

They moved at a good pace, as good as his bad leg allowed. The pain in his muscles, not used to exertion, was nothing compared to the pain in his bones. For as long as he could remember, the one thing he was always able to count on was the strength of his own body. He struggled to deal with this new handicap.

After about three hours of walking, he was forced to accept that they would have to stop to rest.

The rain hadn't started up again yet. That was good. But they hadn't come across any edible fruits all morning, and he was getting hungry. Audrey probably felt the same.

"We'll stop here to eat," he said, and laid his gun against a tree before lowering himself to a fallen log.

She sat next to him with a puzzled expression.

She wasn't going to go for this. Not in a million years. But he didn't have the strength or the time to go off on a hunt. And considering what had happened when he'd left her alone the last time, it was probably a good idea to stick as close to her as possible.

He gave Audrey a reassuring smile, reached for a thick, broken-off branch that lay next to them and lifted it, revealing a scampering jumble of grubs. He picked them quickly, as many as he could before the rest disappeared under the decomposing leaves.

"They have more nutrition in them per pound than vegetables," he said, holding his palm out between them, wishing he could have done better for her.

She stared at the wriggling mess, reached out a tentative hand and pinched a fat white one between her thumb and forefinger, lifted it to her mouth and swallowed it whole, then cleared her throat.

His jaw went slack from surprise.

"You've missed a couple of reality shows since you've been gone." She grinned. "People eat stuff like this on TV now almost every night to win prizes." She went for another grub and sent it after the first.

THE BUGS FREAKED HER OUT, but she wasn't about to show it.

If he could put up with it, and the pain that must have been just about crippling him all morning, then she sure wasn't going to whine. She had seen how he walked, how his limp had gotten more and more pronounced through the morning, the muscles in his face growing tighter and tighter. He was doing this for her, for Nicky, whom he'd never even met. She wasn't going to make his job harder by being difficult. She wasn't going to fuss over a couple of bugs.

The next one had a little dirt on it. Audrey blew off the leaf dust before she put the thing into her mouth. The grub wriggled all the way down but stopped once it reached her stomach.

He waited until she had her fill before he took any, as he had with the meat the night before and the bananas before that. She made sure she didn't take more than her share. With this latest course, it wasn't too difficult.

"Do you think we'll get there in time?" She watched him as he ate methodically, obviously not thinking of the food.

"It'll be close, but if all goes well, yes."

He looked remarkably different without the caveman do, and much younger. With the dreadlocks gone, a lot of the grays disappeared in the short, light brown mess she'd made of his hair. He was nowhere near fifty as she'd thought before—around his midthirties perhaps. He had great lips. Her attention lingered on the strong masculine line of his jaw. The skin that had been until now hidden behind the bushy beard was a shade lighter than the rest, giving the odd impression that he was wearing a mask.

And maybe he was. He had told her very little about himself. She opened her mouth to ask, but changed her mind. If he didn't want to talk about his past, she could respect that. He was helping her save Nicky. That was all she needed to know.

He examined the vegetation around them, got up, broke an eight-inch twig off a tree, brought it over and snapped it in half, offering one of the pieces to her.

"Toothbrush," he said, and started to chew at the end of his.

She followed his example. The bark was bitter but the inner fibers had a mild spicy taste.

"It's good to keep everything as clean as you can." He chucked his stick after a couple of minutes.

They rinsed their mouths, drank and moved on. When the sun reached its highest point in the sky and she noticed he was limping too hard again, she asked if they could stop to rest.

"Right over there." He pointed, and she followed him to a tree with yellow, podlike fruit hanging from it. "I've been hoping we would come across something to eat."

He grabbed a long stick and beat them down, and she picked them up.

"Looks like starfruit." Only smaller. She'd seen those in the grocery store but never had one.

"It is." He sat next to her on the ground and watched her as she took a tentative bite.

"Sweet." With just a hint of sourness in the juicy flesh. She gobbled the rest of the fruit, then grew embarrassed when she realized he was smiling at her fervor.

"Better than the grubs?" The starfruit juice glistened on his lips. A few drops ran down his chin, and he wiped them off with the back of his hand.

She swallowed. "Anything has to be better than grubs."

His mouth tugged up at one corner. "You'd be surprised."

She was about to ask him what he meant, but he tensed and put a finger to his lips.

What? She strained her ears but didn't hear a thing.

He motioned to her to stand and follow him as he examined the trees around them, selecting one that had branches starting low to the ground. He stepped up quickly and pulled her after him, higher and higher, until they could no longer see the ground from the leaves.

He lay on his stomach on the jumble of branches and she did the same, hanging on for dear life. He was watching something, then she spotted the opening in the foliage that gave them a view of what was going on below. A guerilla fighter passed under them, heading straight for the fruit on the ground. He picked up a couple, calling out to others who appeared soon. They gathered the starfruits and took potshots at the ones that remained on the tree.

She was holding on to the branches so tightly she was getting a muscle cramp in her arm, but she didn't dare move. Her blood pounded loudly enough in her ears to drown out half the voices below. She waited, as still as she could. Then a small movement caught her eye a few feet up the branch she was laying on. A spider. Not just any spider, this was the prototype, the mother and father of all spiders, as big as her palm with fingers outstretched. And it was coming toward her.

She had quarter-inch goose bumps, every hair on her body standing on end. She clenched her teeth and watched the beast move closer and closer. It would reach her face first. If she let go of the branch to try to shoo it away, she would fall.

She blew at it gently as it got within a few feet and stopped. It didn't seem to notice. She blew harder.

The fighters were still talking down below. Never a better time to take a break, for heaven's sake. The beast meandered forward a few inches as if trying to figure out what she was.

Eating grubs was one thing, but if Gargantua came another spidy step closer, she was going to get seriously freaked out. No way could she take it if the spider crawled on her face. She needed to think of something else. No matter what happened, she couldn't make a sound, couldn't let go of the branch.

Then she saw Brian's arm come into her field of vision and she looked up just in time to see him scoop up the beast. He placed it gently on a cross branch a good distance from her, and gave it a gentle shove in the opposite direction. Gargantua obeyed.

She was weak from relief, a wet noodle draped over the branch. She owed him. She owed him big.

Then finally the guerillas moved on. Brian waited a couple of minutes before starting to climb down, helping her descend after him. The job required patience, since her knees were still shaking. Her heartbeat was as labored as a marathon runner's.

He slid to the lowest branch with ease. As difficult as walking seemed for him, up in the canopy he moved like the lord of the jungle, having enough upper body strength to spare, allowing him to pull himself up, or lower himself from branch to branch with ease.

He held his hands out, and she thumped down next to him, right in the circle of his arms. She put one hand on his shoulder to steady herself, aware the instant they touched of the muscles beneath her palm, his darkening gaze on her face, his lips a few inches from hers. His eyes really were extraordinary. Fire leapt in them, but she didn't pull away.

She kissed him.

BRIAN FROZE.

Her soft, warm lips pressed against his and short-circuited his brain, sending an electric charge through his body that had sparks buzzing over the surface of his skin. He wanted more, he wanted all of her, with an urgency that stole his breath, but he also recognized the kiss for what it was—a gesture of gratitude and relief. And he would have had to be the worst kind of bastard to take advantage of it.

He pulled back and saw surprise flicker in her eyes before he looked away. Surprise at her own spontaneous gesture, or at his reaction? It didn't matter. He wasn't going there. He couldn't.

He stepped aside and turned, scanning the forest, forcing his brain to focus on finding a path. "We better go."

"I'm sorry." Her voice was small and edged with embarrassment. "I don't know what that was."

He glanced back at her, the touch of pink on her cheeks affecting him as much as the kiss had. "Fun," he said, and made his lips stretch into a semblance of a nonchalant smile he would have given her had they met four years ago. "It's just not a good idea."

"No. No, of course not." She busied herself with brushing off her clothes.

He liked the way she moved. Even in the smallest tasks she managed to seem efficient and purposeful. He couldn't help but remember the long, slim limbs that had mesmerized him when she'd washed herself in the creek. His body responded enthusiastically to the memory.

To punctuate another corporeal need,

his stomach growled, reminding him how little they had eaten. She had to be hungry, too. "We should be able to find some more food if we keep our eyes open. If not sooner, then when we reach the river."

She nodded, her features taking on an expression of steeled determination. She was obviously way out of her comfort zone, but no one could ever tell that by looking at her. Her clothes were soiled with dirt, and marred by a couple of small tears left behind by the thorny vines. But she had zeroed in on their goal and didn't waste time with complaining about things that couldn't be changed.

He had to stop keeping a running list of the things he liked about her. Hell, it was pretty much everything. Liking her and doing something about it were two different things, however. "Ready to move out?"

"Absolutely." She regained her composure enough to flash him a cautious smile.

He really liked the way her eyes crinkled when she smiled.

HAMID LISTENED to his men report back, finishing his rice. No sign of the two that ran away. Where the hell were they?

If it were just the woman, he wouldn't have thought twice about it. But the man bothered him. Jamil's prisoner was a survivor. He had made it through malaria, beatings, years in that damn cage where Jamil had kept him like a pet. He could be halfway to Miri by now. No, maybe not halfway, the woman would slow him down.

They hadn't gone on the river. Omar's men were watching day and night. That was good at least. The jungle would slow them even further, give him more time to act.

He set the bowl down and got up, walked to the crate in the corner. The bombs were ready. They were as powerful as he could make them. But they were no longer safe here. If the man made it out, he could give the army Omar's location. And if Omar was captured, he might give their plan up to save himself.

He called for his men, looked at the two that entered. Good. They were part of the old guard. "You two and your brothers—"

he nodded to the taller one "—will take the crate now."

"To the city?"

He nodded. It was too early, not what they'd planned, but at times like this, flexibility was the key.

"Is Muhammad coming?" the man asked.

"No." Especially not Muhammad. He had caused enough trouble already by bringing western hostages to camp. "You will go quietly. Keep a low profile. Don't stop at any camps. Take enough food. Don't even stop to hunt."

"Of course."

"You stay with the bombs and wait for me."

He would have to go. That part of the plan would have to change, too. Muhammad was too much of a man of impulse, he saw that now. Omar could have gotten the job done, he was eager enough to prove himself to volunteer for any mission. But if something went wrong, would Omar be willing to sacrifice himself for their cause?

Jamil would have, if he could have been

talked into it, but too late to think about that now. Jamil was dead.

Hamid ran his fingers across the top of the crate. He would go. And when the time came, he would do whatever was necessary. First the bombs, to scare out of the country the foreign dogs who supported the current government and its malpractices. Then he would unite all the guerilla groups in the hills—he was making good progress with that—and go head-to-head with the military.

And then his country would finally be free.

THEY WALKED IN SILENCE, picking their way over fallen logs and through leafy bunches of vines that were hanging from the canopy, blocking their way.

"This way," Brian said, wincing at the stab of pain that flashed through his knee every time he put his weight on his bad leg.

The ground was waterlogged, extensive buttress root systems tripping them up, blocking their way. "Look for game trails," he told Audrey. "It's the easiest going, as long as you remember to get off them at dusk. You don't want to run into any night predators."

"Have you ever come across a tiger?"

He glanced back. "The native tribes believe if you speak the word out loud one will appear."

"Oh." She looked around and stepped up until she was right behind him.

He hadn't planned on telling that story to anyone. Wasn't even sure what had really happened. But what the hell. What else did they have to talk about?

"Once," he said, keeping a steady pace. "I think. I could have been hallucinating. I was fighting malaria at the time."

"Was it after you were captured?"

He nodded. "I was pretty much out of it. The fever was so bad Jamil's men didn't even tie me up. I remember coming to in the middle of the night and deciding to escape. I made it about six feet before I collapsed behind some bushes and passed out."

"Were you attacked?"

"It was the strangest thing." He stopped to look at her. "I remember coming around, feeling a hot breath on my face—boy, did it stink. Think dog breath a hundred times over. I looked up into the face of this enormous beast. I thought, this was it, I was finished. And it licked my forehead a couple of times then walked away."

She stared at him, her green eyes round. "It licked you?"

"I'll never forget it. He had a big tongue, rough. Maybe he liked the salt in the sweat." He shrugged.

"Maybe he was tasting you and decided there was something wrong with you and you might make him sick."

"Could be, although predators usually pick the sick and weak of the herd."

"True."

They moved on, and he held a bunch of vines out of the way to let her pass through, brushed off a giant beetle that had fallen on her shoulder before she noticed it.

"Did the tiger get any of the guerillas?"

He shook his head. "They found me in the morning. Never figured it out that I was trying to escape. They thought I went to relieve myself and passed out."

"They didn't keep you in the cage back then?"

"The first year they caught me, we spent on the trails, moving from one makeshift camp to another. Then we came across the place you saw, an abandoned poacher hideaway. It came with a handful of sheds and a tiger cage. Jamil took a liking to it."

"Jamil?"

"The leader before Omar. Omar was the one writing by the fire—short guy with the broken nose."

They walked on in silence for a while. She was probably thinking about the guerillas.

He was thinking about her lips on his.

She was a shock to the system, no doubt about it. He should have felt relieved that she wasn't scared of him, despite his appearance, but all things considered maybe it would have been safer for her if she were.

He would never consciously take advantage of her and their situation, but too much civilization had melted off him over the years, and even he wasn't sure what kind of man had walked out of that cage. He wasn't sure if he knew himself, if he could trust himself. At one point in his life he'd had principles, he had lived by a code. But while in captivity, all that had been replaced by a single objective: survival, for which he would have done absolutely anything.

He fought his way through some bushes and helped her. "We must be nearing the river. The closer we get, the more undergrowth there is."

As bad as visibility was in the jungle— no more than fifty yards—here they could barely see six feet around them. The tall plants gave a feeling of claustrophobia, putting him on edge, on alert for what might jump out at them.

Thankfully, they didn't have to fight the overgrown vegetation long. He spotted a winding trail a few minutes later.

"Deer and wild pigs." He examined the tracks, a jumble of hoofprints pressed into the soft soil.

They still had to duck under vines that hung from the branches above, but the going was a hell of a lot easier.

"How far is the river?" She kept close,

careful not to fall more than a few steps behind.

"Just ahead, can you hear it?"

"No."

"Listen for the fishing birds."

They moved forward at a good pace, the soil growing soggier underfoot as they progressed. With all the rain, the river probably had been flooding a lot lately. High water would make crossing more difficult. On the other hand, dangerous waters meant less river travel, less chance of somebody seeing them.

"This probably will be the most difficult part. Once we get to the other side, things will be easier." He tried to give her something to look forward to.

Crossing a river was risky under the best of circumstances. Walking into floodwaters was sheer insanity.

They came around a bend in the trail and the water was in front of them, rolling slowly, brown with the mud it had washed down from the mountains. He watched drifting wood to gauge the river's speed, looked for white water that would indicate rocks beneath the surface. He picked out a spot on the other side that looked like a good target for landing, considering the current and the thick jumble of plants that covered the bank.

"I didn't realize the river would be this wide," she said behind him.

"It's the rainy season." He turned around and found her watching the water, her face reflecting her doubts. He didn't blame her. Nobody with a smidgen of survival instinct would want to go anywhere near that river.

He hunted around until he found a fallen branch, as thick as his wrist and about six feet long, then looked some more and picked up another, about the same. He stripped off side shoots with his knife, then dropped the two poles at Audrey's feet.

"Shouldn't we look for a better spot to cross?" She eyed the rolling water.

If only they had that luxury.

"Can't afford to waste the time. And we might not find any." He tossed her the rifle then picked a tree with a multitude of vines hanging from its branches and walked to it.

"Better get to work," he called back over his shoulder. "Keep your eyes open."

They were on a well-traveled game trail used by animals to get to the river. A prime hunting location for predators. He wanted to be gone from the spot before nightfall. As rare as tigers were these days, it was always better to err on the side of caution.

He climbed the tree, using the vines for leverage, and cut one thick stem after the other. They had to hurry, and not only so they wouldn't become supper for the local wildlife. They had to cross the river while they still had full daylight to guide them. Waiting until morning was out of the question.

Time was tight.

They couldn't afford to waste any of it if they were to save the hostages.

Chapter Five

Sweat dripped from his eyebrows. Brian wiped his forehead with his shirtsleeve without missing a beat.

Cutting the vines took serious effort, their woodsy fibers hard to sever with a simple knife. A good axe or a hatchet could have done the job in a third of the time. And the more he cut, the duller the blade got from the rough work. He sized up the pile Audrey had carefully uncoiled and stretched on the ground. Should be enough. He climbed down, careful where he stepped.

"Hang on to this." He picked up a good length of vine and handed one end to her, pulled hard on the other to test it.

Now was the time to make sure there

were no rotted sections, or areas where insects and rodents might have weakened the plant. They did the same to the next and the next until they were done, having to throw aside only two.

He sat by the pile and got to work. Audrey settled next to him, her thigh brushing against his when she leaned forward.

Being around her was like swimming in a tank full of electric eels. She zapped his senses, shorted his concentration with every move.

"Can I help?" Her luminous green eyes sparkled in the dappled light.

Go someplace where I can't see you, and take temptation with you.

No, that wasn't fair. It wasn't her fault that he had a hard time keeping his mind and hands off her. He focused on the work in front of them, pushed back the tide of primal urges rising in his blood.

"Like this." He held the ends of two vines together, made a loop and tied them in a secure knot.

She tried with another one and managed pretty well. He tested her knot. It held.

When all the vines were connected, he rechecked every single knot one more time. Then he tied one end of the line around a tree, the other around his waist, grabbed his pole and waded into the water. The river was about a hundred feet wide; he had more than enough "rope" the get him to the other side.

"Feed the line to me little by little. Hold tight if I slip." He walked farther into the murky water, using the pole to probe for holes in the river bottom in front of him.

The silt was soft and slippery. It sucked his boots in, making the crossing difficult.

"When I'm across, untie the line from the tree and tie it around your waist. Use the pole for support," he called back, then turned his attention to crossing.

He moved forward as fast as he could, not only because it was never a good idea to linger in water—too many nasty parasites that could make your life miserable for a long time—but because he hated to leave Audrey unprotected. The sooner they were both on the same side again, the better.

The water was all right, a few degrees

colder than the air. In a few steps he was in to his waist, then his chest and his shoulders. Then the pole no longer reached bottom in front of him. He pushed away from the mud that was sucking his boots in, and began to swim, feeling the line pull tight, then loosen as Audrey gave him some slack.

The closer he got to the middle, the stronger the current grew. He let go of the pole and put everything he had into swimming, careful with the debris the river carried. In what seemed an eternity later, his feet touched semisolid ground again, and he was able to walk, losing his footing a couple of times, but making his way forward steadily.

Without the pole, the going was slower. He had to feel out where he was stepping before putting his weight on his foot. He couldn't afford to slip into a hole and break a leg.

But he reached shore soon enough, his clothes a soggy, muddy mess. He fought the plants that reached into the water and found a spot where he could climb the bank, and untied the line while he was catching his breath. Once he secured it to a tree, he waved to Audrey to follow.

The tight set of her mouth betrayed her nerves. Nothing but determination in her movements, though. She pushed herself to complete the task at hand, as always.

He pulled the line with each step she took forward, more nervous watching her than when he was in the water himself. She was doing well, keeping her head up, using the pole. Then she was swimming. He pulled the line, helping her. She drifted downriver, but the line held and kept her safe.

He only took his eyes off her to look for signs of danger every once in a while, keeping his ears on guard for the sound of approaching boats. They were lucky, it looked like she would make it. She was almost at the point where he figured her feet would start touching bottom again soon.

Then a log in the water upriver caught his attention, and he swore, pulling harder on the vine.

"Swim to shore," he yelled, not caring now who might hear him. She was in more immediate danger from the log than from anyone. If her line got tangled, she'd be trapped. "Go with the current! On your back. Forty-five degrees to shore. Swim backwards." It was the safest position for someone carried away by floodwaters.

He gave her back the whole length of the vine rope, and she understood, stopped fighting to reach shore where he was and let the current take her downriver, just trying to get across enough so the log would float by behind her. She almost cleared it. The log hit the line ten feet or so in front of her. He could see the patched length of vine tangle in the roots as the dead tree bobbed in the water, rolling in the current.

He pulled on the line, desperate. Maybe he could drag her in log and all. *Come on, baby.* But the vine rope didn't budge. He let it go. If it snapped, he would lose her.

Audrey was swimming for the log, probably hoping to hang on to it until they figured out what to do next.

"Keep away from it!"

It would be too easy to get tangled in the line and the roots. The log could roll and push her under. She heard him and stopped, paddling in place, waiting for him to save her.

He wasn't sure he could.

He rushed forward, blood drumming in his ears. Not many things scared him anymore, but watching her struggle at the end of the rope left him petrified.

He had to come up with something. Now.

She had a knife, but if she cut herself loose, without the line the water would carry her downriver. The current was too strong for her to make it to shore without help. If she stayed where she was, her strength would run out sooner or later and she would drown.

He scaled the nearest tree, slashed at the vines, made another line and ran through the forest. He had to reach her before her line snapped.

He was tying knots as he went, having a line less than half the size of the original ready by the time he reached the spot on the bank that was close enough, yet a little above her. That way he could let the current carry him instead of fighting it. He tied himself out and dived in, not bothering with a pole, swimming for her with everything he had. She swam toward him, both of them careful to avoid the log.

His lungs choked with the water he swallowed, but he reached her. "Hang on tight." He cut the vine that held her trapped.

The current grabbed on to the extra weight and pushed them both under for a second. They came up spluttering. He kicked with his feet to stay afloat, grabbed onto the rope, one hand over the other again and again, struggling to pull them in.

The progress was slow, swimming in the strong current with her hanging on to his neck damn near impossible. They spent as much time underwater as above it. But then his feet touched the muddy bottom, and soon hers did, too.

For a moment they clung to each other, standing together against the rage of the river that swirled around them. He barely caught his breath when he heard the spluttering sound of a motor then the next second spotted the boat that came from upriver.

Damn.

He pointed it out to Audrey, took a deep breath, and when he saw her do the same, pulled her under with him. He headed for an overhang of bushes by the bank, going by feel, the water so murky there was no point in opening his eyes. He held her hand tight, came up when he felt the branches with his other hand, pulled her farther in.

"Omar's men?" Audrey whispered against his ear.

Overhanging leaves hid them from view, but they could see the river through the small gaps between branches.

"Poachers."

The boat stopped and the six men inside looked over the tied-out log. One of them killed the motor, scanned both banks. Brian strained to hear what they were saying, but couldn't. Then they tensed, reached for their weapons.

He grabbed his knife under the water, knowing there was little he could do if they spotted his hiding spot. They had guns. Even if he threw the knife well and took one out, the other five would shoot Audrey and him into sieves.

But the men weren't looking at him. Soon they all turned their attention upriver. And then he could hear it, too, the sounds of a motor once again.

The boat that came around the bend was smaller than the poachers', but the four guerillas were better armed, holding semiautomatics instead of hunting rifles. The two groups watched each other warily, neither of them saying a word to the other.

For a moment, the tension was palpable in the air, every man gripping his gun. Then the guerillas floated by. Their small boat carried some kind of a crate, covered with tarp. The men were positioned two in the front, two in the back. He watched them carefully, but didn't recognize any.

The poachers waited a good ten minutes before they followed.

When they were out of sight, Brian waded from under the bushes and, once he made sure it was safe, he signaled to Audrey to follow. They made their way to shore—not an easy task. There was no game trail on this side, the vegetation thick to the point of impenetrable, as the plants fought for light.

He was careful to select the thinnest spot, to bend the branches instead of breaking them, to trample as little as possible. Even when he got past that first barrier, he made a point to walk on moss that would spring back up fast, or on stones, instead of in mud that would leave tracks—in case the guerillas came back later to investigate. Audrey followed his example without having to be told.

Once he was sure they couldn't be seen from the river, he stopped. "Check yourself over." He turned from her. "Let me know if you need help." He ran the odd scene on the river through his mind again. It didn't add up. His instincts bristled.

"I'm glad they didn't get into a fight," Audrey said behind him.

He peeled off his clothes and squeezed the water out, draped them over branches, careful not to put anything on the ground.

"That's just it. The poachers had a better boat and it was loaded. But the guerillas had better weapons. I thought they would attack." His legs and torso were all right, but he had a couple of leeches on each arm, five fatties on his shoulders where they had sneaked under his collar.

Judging by the squeak that came from behind him, they had gotten Audrey, too.

"Help," she said.

He turned and found her staring at two big ones just below the spot where her collarbones met. She still had her underwear on, and the soggy cotton tanktop that hid nothing.

"Don't pull," he said. "Their jaws can get ripped. Anything that stays under your skin ups your chances for an infection." A lighter or some salt would have helped, but they didn't have either. "If you can stand them for another minute or two, they'll get full and fall off on their own. It's the safest."

"Oh, gross."

"So tell me about your sister," he said as one of his *friends* dropped to the ground. He kicked it away with his boot, then looked around for food. A profusion of palm trees grew around the river, but it looked like the wildlife had already gotten to them.

"She's great. She's younger than me, very pretty, very wild. And she is brilliant, working on her Ph.D. in mathematics. If she wasn't my sister, I could really learn to hate her," she joked. "We missed spending time together and she decided to come with me for moral support. She's a teacher so she has the summer off anyway. Trev is always up to his neck in work. They got married last year. Actually, she met Trev at my wedding." The last words were said on a tone slightly different from the rest.

He shook the water out of his boots, scraped off the river mud. "Do you miss your ex?"

She gave him a small, wry smile. "No. I still see him from time to time. Trev and he are close friends." She thought for a moment. "I miss the idea of true love, that it's supposed to last forever through thick and thin. I mean, I know now that the whole thing is just a fantasy. A couple is just two people, and people change, and sometimes they change in different directions. I guess

I miss the innocence of believing that happily-ever-after is possible. My parents are divorced. I always swore that would never happen to me. I hate failing."

He could understand that sentiment. Brian shook out his pants and put them back on. "My father used to say romance was invented by greeting card companies and Hollywood to sell merchandise."

Pain was real, as was violence, the old man had said, and the struggle for survival. There were hormones and pheromones, and good old-fashioned primal sexual instinct, but that was all. Everything else was just stuff people deluded themselves into believing.

His parents had cared for each other and that made for a decent marriage and a fine home for him. But whatever their marriage had been before his father had gone off to war, it was certainly no passionate love affair after. The war had changed him, he used to say. It had changed both of them.

"Here we go."

Her leeches fell off almost at the same time as most of his, and she skipped to step away from them. She reached for the spot on her skin, but he stopped her. "Let it bleed for a while. The blood will cleanse the wound. It'll stop on its own."

He nudged the last leech on his shoulder, and when it let go, he put on his shirt, just as Audrey finished buttoning hers.

"Aren't you worried about blood loss?" She looked at him.

"A handful of leeches don't take enough to be concerned over."

"They're still nasty." Her voice was thick with revulsion.

"We better get going. We have to find a place to camp before nightfall. Tomorrow's gonna be a rough day. But if we keep a good pace, we'll be at Hamid's camp by tomorrow night."

She nodded and followed him without complaints. They walked upriver, at enough distance from the muddy bank to avoid leaving tracks and keep out of the dense undergrowth that grew there. He cut back to the water only twice, to remove the two vine ropes from the palms and toss them into the river.

Something about those guerillas didn't sit right with him. They might yet come back to look for the poachers. He didn't want them to find his and Audrey's tracks instead.

FIRE MADE all the difference. The smoke repelled the bugs, the heat kept the chill of the night at bay. Audrey picked the last of the meat off the fish bones. Compared to the bitter roots they had existed on all day, the meal seemed like an extravagant treat. Thanks to Brian.

He sat across from her, engrossed in making more hooks from bone. His clothes were drying on the bushes, side by side with hers. Since it wasn't raining for once, they were aiming for a dry night with dry clothes and some sleep in comfort. Their boots hung upside down, speared on three-foot-tall sticks to keep them off the ground and away from bugs. Brian had sprinkled the perimeter of their small camp with ashes to keep crawling insects away. Ants hated ashes, apparently, as did a number of their other bugsy friends.

If you had to be stuck in the jungle, this was the man to do it with. Audrey stood to stretch her legs, her eyes straying to his shoulders, the way the firelight played on the muscles that flexed when he put pressure on his knife. His hands were steady. She only remembered seeing them shake a couple of times today. Amazing what two days of freedom did to the man.

He was transforming slowly, in front of her eyes. He was moving better, his legs getting accustomed to walking. Even his gestures and the way he carried himself were changing. She could have sworn he had grown taller, although it was probably an illusion. He was walking straighter, his body growing used to being free from the confines of the cage.

"How old are you?" she asked, then regretted it. The question would probably make him think of the years he'd lost. "You don't have to answer. Never mind."

"What's today?"

She left the hotel a week ago. "The seventh. August," she added.

He raised his gaze to her, his expression

inscrutable. "I turned thirty-one last month."

She stared at him. "I'll be thirty-one this fall."

They were the same age. It drove home the horror he must have been living in the past couple of years. When she had first seen him, she had thought him old enough to be her father. Even now— She would have definitely not guessed him to be thirty-one.

It wasn't his body—that looked powerful, ageless. She let her gaze slide over the wide shoulders again and the well-muscled arms, the flat stomach, then glanced away when she got to his underwear—if it could be called that—the handmade piece was little more than a loincloth.

The illusion of age came from the ever-present shadow on his face, and in his brilliant blue eyes. Eyes that said they'd seen too much.

She'd glimpsed eyes like that before at the clinic, seen the men and women who had tried to escape their memories by hiding behind drugs or alcohol. Half the people she'd admitted had had some history of severe trauma, physical or sexual abuse, rape, war. A handful of veterans were in residence at any given time.

Brian fed the fire.

Where would his past take him? He had such a strength, not just of his body, but a steel core inside.

He met her gaze, and she looked away.

She shook their clothes out, turned them on the branches to bring the wet sides closer to the fire. A wad of crumpled papers fell out of his pocket. "What's this?"

"Probably Omar's shopping list. It got wet before I had a chance to read it. I can read words here and there. None of it makes any sense. I kept them to use as tinder, but they never had a chance to dry out."

"Do you speak Malay?"

He nodded. "I picked up some over the years."

She flipped through the pages, her gaze settling on what looked like numbers. She pulled closer to the fire. If she looked at it from just the right angle... "There's a date here."

"Yeah?" Brian went back to carving, not looking too excited.

"August ten."

"Maybe he was asking Hamid to a meeting, although—" He set the hook aside and reached for the papers.

"What?"

"The guerillas don't exactly schedule like businessmen. It's always *in a few days,* or *after the monsoon.* They have a different sense of time here in the jungle. Giving or taking a day doesn't matter much. Hell, most of the time they probably don't even know what day it is."

"What's KL?" She scrutinized the paper over his shoulder.

"Where?"

She pointed.

"Damn."

"What?"

"I thought it was a blotch. KL is what the locals call Kuala Lumpur, the capital. Nobody but tourists say the full name."

He riffled through the pages. Silence stretched to a minute, then two.

"Are you thinking what I'm thinking?"

He turned to look at her. "The crate in the boat."

She nodded.

"Maybe the guerillas didn't shoot at the poachers because they couldn't risk return fire."

"Makes sense if the crate was full of explosives."

"Or maybe they were just in a hurry to get somewhere."

She tilted her head. "Kuala Lumpur, August tenth?"

He came to his feet and put on his pants. "When we get to Hamid's camp, we'll radio it in. "

"Do you think they're planning an attack?"

"A couple of days ago, I would have said no. Going after civilians wasn't Jamil's M.O. and Hamid wouldn't have done something this major without his support. But now…" He shrugged. "Omar is just hotheaded and bloodthirsty enough. He wants to make a name for himself. He wants to bring the fight to the next level. He probably has some kind of an agreement with Hamid. It makes sense." He stared into the fire, his expression pensive.

"This is major, isn't it?"

He nodded. "There've been changes. Talk. I don't know—a feeling around camp. Too much coming and going. I knew something was up, but I thought it was just Omar, trying to figure out a way to get himself to the top. If we are right and there's an attack planned in KL, it could be just the opening act. Omar and Hamid are both in on it. What if the others are, too? What if this is the beginning of a major offensive?"

"We have to let someone know."

"We can't be still in the jungle when it happens, that's for sure. I have a feeling the Royal Malaysian Air Force will retaliate by bombing the hell out of this patch of the island."

She checked her clothes, found them dry and put them on, except for the socks. Brian had warned her to let her feet breathe at night.

It said something about the man that he took care to explain the smallest things to help her avoid discomfort. He had been giving her a crash course on jungle survival as they'd walked, giving her his vote of confidence that she would remember and could handle things. Instead of treating her like a clueless burden, he related to her as an equal—a teammate. She appreciated that.

"So what do we do now?" she asked.

"Get as much sleep as we can, then start out at first light. Hamid probably has a satellite phone or radio. We'll call in what we know."

Chapter Six

The rain had started toward dawn and forgot to stop. Although they kept close to the river, there was no point trying to get a fish for lunch—lighting a fire was out of the question. They ate grubs and whatever fruit they could find as they walked, boots sticking in the mud.

Starting midafternoon they started to check the water's edge more and more often, fighting the dense vegetation to get to it. Then they came across the spot they were looking for—a narrow area where the bushes had been cleared. Brian looked over the two motorboats pulled up on shore.

He watched the trail from the cover of the bushes, and when he was certain it was deserted, turned back to Audrey, who squatted behind him.

"I have to go check out the camp while there's still daylight to see."

She rose, ready to follow him wherever he would lead her. Her blind trust in him was gratifying and frightening at the same time. What the hell was he supposed to do with her? She'd be in danger if she came with him and she'd be in danger if he left her here alone. There was no safe spot for an untrained civilian in the jungle.

"What's wrong?" She blinked away the raindrops that clung to her eyelashes, squinting, puzzled at his hesitation.

She looked like a drowned mouse. She looked gorgeous. He'd had beautiful women at one time in his life, although his relationships had tended to be as brief as they were few and far between. One girl had accused him of missing the bonding gene. She had been right. He barely remembered her, other than that she'd been fun-loving and easy.

"I can't believe we're finally here. We're going to get Nicky back today."

He nodded. There was nothing easy about Audrey Benedict.

He motioned to her to stick to him as he followed the trail at a distance from the forest.

Unlike Omar's camp, Hamid's was much bigger than just a clearing in the jungle. Shacks spread up the hillside, with a large steel-frame building dominating the landscape, a gray satellite dish on top outlined against the green background. He could see all manner of industrial equipment, rusting, overrun by vines, in the process of being reclaimed by the jungle.

"An abandoned mine," he whispered to Audrey, keeping behind the bushes as he eyed the structures. There was nobody outside, and he couldn't blame them, the rain was coming down pretty hard. He could see shadows moving in several windows. They were watching.

He tensed when the door of one of the sheds opened, but the man who came out sprinted to another building without looking their way.

"Come on." He kept low as he moved

ahead, circling the camp. They had to get the layout before night fell.

"How many of them do you think there are?" Audrey kept close behind.

With everyone inside, it was hard to tell. The rain complicated things. From the size of the dozen or so huts, he figured about fifty men. Of course, half the huts might be empty or, on the other hand, there might be many more guerillas, hiding from the weather in some mine shaft. There could be an army underground, the mine could probably hold hundreds. But he didn't think so.

Hamid's men had visited Jamil from time to time. His impression was that their group was larger than the one that held him captive, but not by much.

"Four, maybe five dozen." He gave her his best bet, seeing no sense in sugarcoating things. Better for her to know what they were facing, better to be prepared for it.

"Do you think the hostages…" She looked at him, her voice rough with worry.

"I'm sure they're still alive. Hamid is a professional at this kind of thing. They're probably in little danger until the deadline is up tomorrow."

Even after that, the man wouldn't kill all of them. Just one or two to show everyone he was serious, then he would probably set another deadline for the rest. Brian judged the distance between the buildings, tried to see if there was a way to get into the big one without having to use the front door that was most likely guarded.

He had a feeling that's where the hostages were. Somewhere down the mine, not the most ideal location for a rescue operation—like going to fight a bear in his cave. Getting trapped would be all too easy, and Hamid's men would have the home advantage. They knew every tunnel, while he would be fighting blind.

And alone. No way was he going to take Audrey in there with him.

He moved on, memorizing the terrain, careful to note distances, the position of the huts. There was very little activity. If the men moved around more he could have gotten a better handle on their number, but everyone seemed content to stick out the miserable weather inside.

Dusk came on them fast.

"Let's go while we can still see." He backed away, not wanting to waste time with fumbling around in the dark.

Hamid and his men were in for the night. Time to start putting his plans in action. They went back to the river, using the trail this time, listening for anything suspicious.

"Help me with this," he said when they got to the spot they'd found earlier. He heaved against one of the motorboats, pushing it into the water.

"Where are we going?" Audrey gave it her best effort as always, and the boat slipped into the river with ease.

"Just down a little. Get in." He helped her, then pushed out the boat even farther before pulling himself over the side. He grabbed the pole lying in the bottom and used it to give the vessel direction.

"I want the boats somewhere where we can get to them quickly, somewhere they wouldn't be looking for them when they come after us." He didn't turn the motor on, but let the river carry them. "What does your sister look like?"

"She's my height, short blond hair, skinny. She works out like a banshee. You're not going to have to worry about her keeping up unless she's injured."

The last couple of words came out shaky.

"She's fine. Hamid treats his hostages well. To him they're merchandise. He'd want to keep them in sellable condition."

She didn't respond to that, and her silence got to him more than if she had thrown a crying fit. There were words, he was sure of it, that someone who knew them could have spoken to comfort her. But it wasn't him. It filled him with an impotent anger he recognized as useless, so he forced his mind back to the hillside, to the camp, planning his route and course of action.

When they got a good two hundred feet from the trail, he jumped out and pulled the boat to shore, pushing it up on the slick mud into the cover of the overhanging vines and bushes. They scratched the hell out of his hands, but he ignored the pain, a minor irritation compared to his leg that was torturing him at full throttle.

Darkness fell by the time they were done. Getting back into the water without being able to see what debris was coming at him would be a reckless move, but he didn't have a choice. He had to get the second boat. Even if, God forbid, not all of the hostages were able to make it this far, he couldn't leave that one for the guerillas to follow in.

"Stay here. I'll bring over the other boat." He handed Audrey the rifle. "You keep this."

He hated to leave her alone, remembering well what had happened the last time she'd been left with the gun to fend for herself. And she was probably remembering, too.

"Nobody goes outside in weather like this, especially not at night," he tried to reassure her.

He couldn't see her face, but could see enough of her silhouette to know she was straightening her spine. He smiled into the darkness. *That's my girl.*

"Be careful," she said.

He reached out, but stopped short of caressing her face, waved a lame farewell instead and turned into the woods. Rain pelted him from above, his progress slower than he would have liked on the muddy, slippery ground.

He thought of Audrey behind him and the hos-tages ahead, the lives that depended on him. How the hell did that happen? He wasn't sure if he was up for the task. He was a broken man, and not just his bad leg. He was way out of practice. It was too much responsibility, more than he was prepared for. Still, quitting wasn't in his nature. He had to try.

He reached the boat, pushed it into the water and floated down the swollen river with a fair speed. The darkness was complete, he was going by feel. Then he heard the most fake birdcall he'd ever heard in his life. And a minute later he heard it again. He grabbed the pole and pushed the boat toward the sound, letting Audrey guide him to a safe landing.

"You're a regular nightingale. Any other

hidden talents?" He jumped out, and she was right there, helping.

"I can wiggle my ears." She pulled on the boat.

The woman wasn't afraid of work, that was for sure. Come to think of it, she wasn't afraid of much.

"Did you run into any trouble?" she asked.

"Not yet. But I have a feeling I'll be coming across some soon." He tied the second boat to a nearby palm tree, next to the first. He wasted no time, but climbed the palm and hacked off a good pile of leaves.

"I want you to stay here," he said after he skidded down. "Cover the boats so they don't fill up with rain." He could have turned them over, but he wanted them to be ready to jump in, had a feeling they would be leaving in a hurry. "Keep the gun. Don't be afraid to use it."

This time when he reached out, he did touch her, drew his crooked index finger over her wet cheek. "If I'm not back by daybreak, get into one of the boats and go downriver. Let the current float you, don't turn on the motor unless someone notices you and they give chase. Keep down. Make every bullet count."

"You need it more." She pushed the rifle toward him.

"It's not up for discussion," he said, and heard her long draw of breath.

"Okay."

She was smart enough to know that fighting over this would waste precious time.

"Do you want the bank statement?"

A second passed before he remembered what she was talking about. "Audrey, I'm not going there to negotiate."

He was bringing back all the hostages, or as many as he could, and he meant to push Hamid for an explanation of Omar's message. Although he had a date, Kuala Lumpur was a major metropolis. To prevent an attack, the government would need an exact location. Damn, it was a tall order—a tough operation he wasn't sure he was fit to attempt. But he was going to do it anyway.

The job was in his blood, trained into him—complete the rescue, save the weak. He had no fear for himself, no hesitation on that score, and he was glad to discover that here was at last some deep part of him that the guerillas didn't manage to take away, couldn't beat out. It was a fragment he recognized, something he could maybe build on to regain the rest.

She reached out a hand in the darkness and put it over his that somehow had come to cradle her face. "Be careful," she said again, with tremors in her voice this time.

That got to him. She was scared, and there was little he could do to protect her. He couldn't be in two places at the same time. He should have been able to offer some reassurance and comfort, but saying "you'll be fine" just didn't seem enough.

He stepped forward and enfolded her in his arms awkwardly, the gun between them. "I'll be back for you," he said, surprised at his own reluctance to move away.

She leaned her forehead against his chin. "I know."

It would have been the most natural thing to press his lips against the crown of her hair, but he couldn't do it. Instead, he walked away.

His mind was full of her, every cell of his brain, all his senses. His nose was full of her wet scent, her last words still ringing in his ears. God, he was pitiful. Thinking about her instead of what he was about to do was a surefire way of getting them both killed.

The mission. He refocused his mind, alert once again as he moved forward in the jungle. He could barely see a foot or two in front of him, any noise an enemy might have made was drowned out by the rain. He was deaf and blind, in enemy territory, without as much as a gun. But he wasn't unarmed. He'd been a soldier an awful long time. He had his instincts.

He kept close enough to the river to let the sound of the water guide him, then once he reached the trail that led to camp, he followed that. He moved off it just before he reached the hillside camp, creeping forward slowly. Not that he was too concerned about running into anybody, but he was concerned about taking a wrong step and rolling down into a ravine, sinking into a rabbit hole and breaking a leg.

He reached camp after a couple of minutes. Lights shone in the windows, except for one shack. He kept in the shadows and stole closer to that one. He peeked in through the cracks in the wall, not wanting to put himself in line with the window. Just because the light wasn't on, it didn't mean nobody was in there.

But he lucked out. He could see the outlines of two people inside, both lying down. They were silent and unmoving. Good. He crept to the door, tried it. Unlocked. Which meant the two weren't hostages. He opened the door a fraction of an inch at a time then ducked inside, waited until his eyes further adjusted to the darkness.

He put his hand over the mouth of the first guerilla, his knife to his throat. The man woke with a start and grabbed for his wrist. Definitely not a hostage then, his hands hadn't been tied. Brian slit the man's throat and moved on to the other one.

When he was done, he tucked the man's handgun into his waistband, threw the two rifles over his shoulder. He pocketed the box of matches from the table on the way out.

He moved on to the next shack, looked inside. Four men there, playing cards, their guns within easy reach. He could have picked them off with a rifle, but didn't yet want to alert the whole camp to his presence. He waited, ducked deeper into the shadows when the door of another hut opened, then moved forward, keeping an eye on the fighter outlined by the hut's light. The man fumbled with his pants.

Damn. The guy was just taking a piss. He had hoped the fighter was on his way to another hut. But with the door open behind him, Brian couldn't take him out. He would have been in plain sight of everyone inside. Then someone in the hut swore, complaining about the rain blowing in, and the door slammed shut.

He was there in seconds. He held the man so he wouldn't make a noise when he fell, dragged the body into the bushes in the back.

He risked a peek through the window that was partially obscured by vines. Two people remained inside. He could handle that. He left the rifles outside, put on the dead man's hat and shirt, stepped into the hut with his head down, one hand clutching the front of the blood-soaked shirtfront. The men came to their feet at once and stepped toward him, talking over each other. Both hands moving simultaneously, he cut the one on the right, and had his fingers wound around the throat of the one on the left. A minute passed before the guy stopped kicking.

Brian blew out the light, not wanting anyone to see the three dead bodies on the floor should they walk by outside. He discarded the bloody shirt, grabbed whatever weapons he could find, then moved on to the next hut.

Empty. He filled his pockets from the crate of hand grenades he found. He moved from hut to hut and did his job methodically. Search and destroy. The fighters that came at him ceased to be people. They were enemy combatants.

He pushed on until everything that he could do in silence had been done, then dumped his loot of weapons into the bushes, keeping one rifle and one handgun.

Only four of the huts had guerillas in them now, each having more men inside than he could have handled without breaking the silence—nineteen altogether. He would worry about them on the way out.

Time to find the hostages.

He moved toward the main building that at one point must have been the entrance to the mine. There were a number of abandoned mines on Borneo; the island used to be rich in both tin and gold. He'd been in three of them within the first days his team had been dropped into the jungle—before he'd gotten blown up and captured.

Brian reached the corner of the tattered building and crawled under the raised floor, on his back in the mud, ignoring the insects that crawled over him, hoping none of them was fatally poisonous, praying he wasn't crawling into a nest of snakes. He pushed forward slowly, inch by inch, giving whatever lived under there time to get out of his way.

He could see the space above through the cracks in the bamboo floor. Six men— two sleeping, the rest talking. They were complaining about the weather. There were plenty of weapons in sight, each man's rifle within easy reach. He scanned the room, his attention settling on the table, on the pot of rice and pile of bones. His stomach growled, and he tensed, but nobody seemed to have heard him. He turned his head, spotted an opening that looked like it led to a tunnel at the back of the building. There we go. The way to get into the mine.

He crawled from under the building with the same careful deliberation as when he'd gotten in, brushed the bugs off and crept to the hut with the most guerillas in it. The five men were still up, arguing, cleaning weapons. Brian pulled the ring from one of the grenades and shoved it under the raised floor, dashed toward the bushes by the main building.

The explosion shook the hillside and brought plenty of men running, those who were still alive in the other huts and the six from the main building. He ducked inside, noted the large case of explosives by the door, hid behind a bed as he heard boots on stone—more men running up from the mine. He counted eight of them. When they were gone, he grabbed a flashlight and entered the shaft.

The floor was steep. He ran, putting his weight on the front of his feet to make as little noise as possible. Then he heard sounds ahead, nearing, and he ducked into a side passage and let another group of men pass. He didn't want to get into a gunfight yet, didn't want to alert those who guarded the hostages that he was coming. How many guerillas were still down there? Where were the tourists?

Finding them quickly was key. He had to get them up to the surface before the men in the camp above realized he was down here. He didn't like the explosives they had. It would be too easy to collapse the main tunnel and trap everyone below, buried alive.

He rushed forward and came to a door, solid metal. For a moment he considered a grenade to throw off the men on the other side, give him a chance to take a couple out before they got their bearings. But he still didn't know where the hostages were. He couldn't risk harming them. They could be hidden somewhere deep in the myriad tunnels, or they could be just on the other side of this door. The latter would be nice. He didn't have much time to look for them.

He kicked the door open, rifle raised in front of him.

And found himself face-to-face with Hamid and twenty of his men, armed to the teeth.

THE RAIN WAS COMING DOWN pretty hard, the river was rising. Audrey couldn't see it, but she'd had to move back three times now when the water reached her feet.

Had Brian made it to the camp yet? She strained her ears for the sound of gunfire, but couldn't hear anything. It seemed impossible that he would succeed. She'd seen the camp. The force he would meet would be overwhelming. She shouldn't have dragged him into this. She had sent him into sure death.

He had insisted on helping her. What pushed him forward? What made him override the instinct of self-preservation in the interest of others? She wondered if he regretted ever having met her. If it wasn't for her, he would have been halfway out of the jungle by now.

And then it occurred to her that they hadn't simply "met." He had saved her, choosing to risk his own freedom, his own life. He had made the decision selflessly, expecting nothing in return.

Despite his battered appearance, there was a strength in the man as she had never seen before. Tremendous courage, and yet vulnerability, too. And as little as they knew each other, she felt herself respond to him.

She kept her hands on the ropes that held the boats. One of the lines moved, grew taut. The water was high enough to lift that boat. The rope held, but she worried.

She planted her boots firmly in the muddy ground and pulled, managed to make some progress, felt as the bottom of the boat scraped into the mud, but no matter how much she struggled, she couldn't get it out of the water. The second she relaxed her arms, the water took the boat again, and when it did, the side banged against a rock a few feet ahead of her. *Bang.* She yanked at the rope, but the river had the boat now. *Bang. Bang. Bang.*

She waded into the water, wanting to put herself between the boat and the rock, to at least keep it quiet, keep from being discovered. She grabbed the side of the other boat for support, and felt it wobble. The water was taking this one, too.

Bang. Bang. Bang.

She couldn't let both boats slip into the water. She wasn't sure how long the ropes would hold, how long the palm tree would make it once the river was high enough and the current and debris started to push against the trunk. She took off her rifle and threw it inside, grabbed the hull and pulled with everything she had, made some progress, infuriatingly slow, but the boat did slide forward, inch by miserable inch.

Bang. Bang. Bang.

She pulled until her shoulders ached, until she was breathing hard, sweat mixing with rain on her face. But she got the boat to higher ground, untied its rope from the palm tree and tied it up again to a tree a couple of yards farther into the woods.

She waded into the water for the other boat, got in up to her chest before she reached it and realized she could do little. She had to untie it, let it move past the rock and tie it up again. Pulling it out of the water at this stage was beyond her strength.

Using the rope to guide her, she made her way back to the palm tree, fighting against the might of the river that tried to take her with it. Nothing else mattered now but the next step, the next few inches to grab onto the rope. She lost track of time, concentrating on her footing, making her aching arms work harder than she'd ever thought they could.

She reached the palm and found it standing in water now, the rope just below the surface. She tore at the swollen fibers but couldn't untie it.

Bang. Bang. Bang.

She had to do something. They were too close to camp. The rain dampened sound, but the clanging of the aluminum boat against the rock was just loud enough so she couldn't be sure how far it would be heard.

She wrapped her left arm around the rope, grabbed on, then with her right arm pulled her knife and sawed through the knot. The next instant the current caught the boat and it lurched forward, pulling her into the water. She fell face first, went under.

Freed finally, the boat was dragging her out into the deep water. It would drag her on, drown her, if she weren't careful. She came up sputtering but refused to let go. She had lost her knife and hung on to the rope with both hands now. But her strength was no match for the raging river.

She went under again, came up, coughing up water, struggling for air. She had only one choice, one thing to do if she wanted to live. She had to let go of the boat.

Tears stung her eyes as she relaxed her fingers and felt the rope slip from her. She struggled to reach shore, got knocked under by a jumble of branches rushing down-river, but she got back up again. Nicky was out there somewhere, and Brian. And they needed her, counted on her. She had to make it.

She'd lost her hat. Rain pelted her hard from above. She could see little to begin with, the water running into her eyes making things worse. She could make out land, just barely, only because the sky was a miniscule fraction darker above it then above the river.

Swim.

One hand in front of the other.

Her boots were pulling her down, but she kicked wildly, refusing to give up. She had to make it. It wasn't just her life at stake. Others counted on her.

She went under, fought her way up again, coughed up the nasty tasting water. *Kick. Left arm. Right arm. Breathe.*

She wasn't making any progress, nothing but exhaustion to show for her efforts. Then she remembered Brian's words when they'd crossed the river before, and she flipped on her back, swam for shore at an angle.

She was shaking with fatigue by the time she reached shore and collapsed onto the muddy bank, letting the rain wash over her face.

She had lost the boat. Their way to safety.

It was one thing for Brian and her to try to walk out of the jungle. Taking a dozen hostages with them on foot, some of whom might be sick or injured, was another matter. How on earth would they find food for so many people? They had barely found enough by scavenging as they went, to feed the two of them.

An explosion shook the air, coming from the direction of the hillside camp. Brian was out there, fighting guerillas, and she had his gun. Even if by some miracle he succeeded and brought the hostages with him here to their meeting point, one boat would not carry them all. Half of them would be trapped between the river and the pursuing guerillas.

She had to go and warn him.

Her teeth were chattering, her wet clothes pasted to her body, chilling her in the night air. Or was she getting some kind of fever? Didn't matter, couldn't worry about that now. The shakes probably came from the shock of having nearly drowned.

Audrey pulled herself up and dragged her exhausted body forward, feeling around in the dark. She had to find the remaining boat and the gun, and then she had to find Brian.

Chapter Seven

Brian ignored the rifles pointed at him and kept his on Hamid. "Give me the hostages. You're not going to get the money anyway. You took too many this time, foreigners. The government has gotten involved."

He scanned the room, if the place could be called that, walls carved from rock, the crates that stood in for furniture, his eyes hesitating briefly on the only other exit.

"The government doesn't know its head from its ass." The leader seemed calmer than his men, his words slow, deliberate. He had a handgun tucked into his waistband, but he hadn't reached for it. An elaborate tattoo decorated his arm—a leaping tiger with a crown on its head.

"The army has you surrounded." If there ever was a time to bluff, this was it.

The man paused, his small brown eyes watching Brian sharply. "Why aren't they here?"

"I'm here. I'm the negotiator." And the recon team, the main force, and the backup.

"An American?" Hamid said the words with derision and made a dismissing motion with his hand.

But as relaxed as he seemed, tension was thick in the air. Brian looked at the men, making eye contact with one after the other, trying to determine which ones were scared, which ones were angry, if any of them might get nervous enough to shoot without waiting for an order from the boss.

When he turned back to Hamid, he made sure his voice was calm and even. "You kidnapped some Americans. Our governments are working together. Let the tourists go, they don't matter to you. Why die for them? Stay alive to fight for your cause."

Silence followed his words, the sounds

of gunfire barely filtering down to where they were. Hamid's men were probably firing blindly into the jungle, but their panicked incompetence played right into Brian's hands, making it sound as if a good-sized battle raged above.

Hamid tapped his fingers on his gun belt. "What's in it for me?"

Brian relaxed a little. Good. The man was willing to negotiate. "They'll treat you like a political prisoner instead of a criminal."

The man laughed. "One prison is the same as the other. If I let the tourists go free, I go free, too."

Brian shook his head, determined to play out his ruse. "Not gonna happen." If he offered something that was too good to believe, Hamid would become suspicious. They stared at each other for a while before he spoke again. "The army came up the river by boat. No place to land a helicopter around here."

"So?"

"They'll have to take you back to the river. It's the middle of the night. If you run into the jungle, they will never find you."

The man thought on that for a while. "Why are you telling me this?"

"I don't care what happens to you. I get the American hostages home alive, my government will be happy with me, I get a promotion, the wife will be happy. End of story."

Hamid watched him closely. "I could give you a promotion."

Yeah, he probably could. He probably had money stashed away to finance his projects. "No can do, man. I'm the negotiator. I came down here, I have to come up with hostages."

"You don't look like a negotiator." Hamid glanced at his worn clothes.

"I got pulled off another job. Didn't have time to go home and change." He smiled at the man. "It's not your regular nine-to-five type of work. You should understand."

Hamid waited, looked him over again, shook his head. "I don't believe you."

It would have been too easy, Brian thought a split second before the guerilla leader nodded to his men, and all hell broke loose.

Brian ducked behind a metal desk, clipped Hamid in the shoulder on the way. The man went down. Brian let some bullets fly then took cover again. A couple of the men were helping Hamid escape, the rest were shooting back. But Brian was the better shot. He had the room under control in five minutes.

He kicked in the door in the back of the room, grabbed a flashlight, ran down the mineshaft. The hostages were a good three-hundred feet in, tied arms and legs, six Westerners, four Japanese, two Indian and an Orang Ulu man—a local tribesman Brian figured must have been their tour guide. Brian cut the ropes off him then handed him the knife to free the rest while he looked around, hoping to find another way to exit the mine. Nothing. The other end of the shaft was closed in.

"Which one of you is Nicky?" he asked when he stepped back to the hostages.

A petite blond stood up by the wall. He ran the flashlight over her face. She was Audrey's sister all right, same eyes, same determined set of the mouth.

"Your sister loves you very much," he told her, then helped the last person shrug off his ropes. "Let's go, people."

They followed him into the large room where he had fought with Hamid's men. Some of the women sobbed at the sight of the bodies that littered the floor. He didn't have time to worry about them.

"Everyone who knows how to shoot a gun, grab one," he said and riffled through the desk, stuffed handfuls of papers into his shirt before moving on.

He went ahead to check out the main building, but found it empty. Not for long. Soon Hamid's men would figure out there was no army shooting back from the forest and they would come back for him.

Except someone *was* shooting back. He stilled. Through the window, he caught a glimpse of a flash of gunfire that came from the bushes, directed toward camp. What the hell?

Audrey.

It had to be her. What the hell was she thinking?

She was no coward, and he liked that

about her, but she had to learn to obey orders from a team leader when she was in a team operation. And he was the team leader here, damn it.

"Let's go. Keep down, get away from this building as fast as you can, too much explosives in here. Go to the right, into the jungle, and wait for me." He turned to the Orang Ulu man. "You take care of them. Don't leave."

"No, sir."

"What can I do?" One of the American men stepped forward, rifle in hand. He didn't seem happy that Brian had given lead to a mere native.

"You follow him." Brian jerked his head toward the tribesman. "Keep quiet, make sure everyone stays together. Your life depends on it."

"I'll take care of them. Don't worry about it. Those sons of bitches out there have it coming—"

"Your job is not to get revenge on the guerillas. You just focus on staying alive. Got it?" He waited until the man reluctantly nodded.

He scanned the rest of the group, noted who took weapons and who didn't. "Don't shoot unless you're shot at. Otherwise you'll just draw attention to yourselves," he told them, and hoped to hell they were paying attention.

The night and the rain made for poor visibility, working in their favor. Brian killed the light then stepped outside. Using up the hand grenades in his pocket, he covered for the hostages until they disappeared into the trees. Then he headed for Audrey. Damn it. He'd told her to stay put. Now he had to get her and scatter the remaining guerillas before he could come back to use the radio.

He crouched and just began to cut across the clearing when a group of men came around the side of the building, guns blazing. He threw himself on his stomach and did the best he could, but was nowhere near cover. Bullets slammed into the ground around him. Hard to shoot back without risking hitting the building—he was too close. If the explosives blew, he had a better than good chance he would blow with them.

He crawled backward, using careful aim. Then someone from behind him sprayed the men with bullets, and the next second he was blinded and deafened by a ground-shaking explosion.

He felt a pair of hands on his ankles, somebody pulling him toward the jungle. The gunfire had stopped.

"Audrey?" He twisted onto his back.

She let go of his legs and reached for his hands to help him up. "Are you okay?"

He nodded.

"Did you find Nicky?"

"She's waiting for us in the forest with the rest." He grabbed her and dragged her into the woods, into the cover of one of the larger trees, then leaning against the trunk crushed her to him, holding her for a long moment, feeling her heart beat against his chest. She was unharmed. Alive. "What the hell are you doing here?"

She lifted her head, hesitated before responding. "The river took one of the boats."

AUDREY CRINGED. She should have done more, fought harder against the river. Their lives depended on their ability to get away. But under the considerable guilt, a current of joy spread through her veins, and hope. Nicky was alive and free.

"The other one?" Brian asked as he moved forward carefully.

What? Oh, the other boat. "I pulled it to higher ground. The water is rising fast." She kept close behind him.

"Must be raining even harder up the mountain."

"Did you radio for help?"

He didn't say anything for a while. "You blew up the radio."

Oh, God. First the boat and now the radio.

He swore under his breath.

She waited for him to yell at her, to tell her she had practically sentenced them all to death. But instead, he stopped, raising his hands to signal for her to do the same.

She listened, but couldn't hear anything over the rain.

"Don't shoot," he called out.

The next second bullets flew into the trees a few feet to their left.

He pushed her down, flattened her into

the mud, half-covering her with his body. The forest fell silent. "Don't shoot," he said again, his voice clipped with anger.

There was some scuffle ahead, people talking.

"Nicky," she said, hope making her voice thick.

And she could see a shadow separate from a tree, and heard her name called and she was on her feet, rushing forward into her sister's arms, the rain washing away her tears as fast as they formed. "Nicky."

"How did you get here?"

"Are you all right?" They spoke at the same time.

"Did they hurt you?" she asked, holding her breath until Nicky shook her head.

Brian was right there. "We have to move out."

And she could see the rest of the people now, the darker shapes in the dark of the jungle, coming forward one after the other.

"What the hell did you think you were doing?" Brian was chewing out one of them.

"Hey." The man stood his ground, not bothering to keep his voice down. "You sent us into the jungle. We didn't know if you were coming back or not. I have the right to defend myself, same as everybody."

Brian was silent. Ominously so. He was close enough so she could feel the anger radiate from his body. Audrey detangled herself from her sister and stepped between the two men. "We have to get going."

"He could have killed you," Brian said.

She'd never heard his voice so tight. "I'm fine. Everyone is fine."

He stepped away. "Follow me closely, watch where you step, it's slippery. Make as little noise as possible. There are still plenty of guerillas out there," he told the group, then turned and started out.

Nicky came up behind her and took her hand. Audrey squeezed it, as they followed him.

"Who is he?" her sister asked close to her ear.

"Some kind of special forces," she whispered back. "He saved my life, Nicky. He saved all of us."

"He's scary."

She smiled. She'd had the same first impression of him. It seemed a lifetime ago. She shook her head in the darkness. "He is a hero."

"Where's Trev?"

"He sent the money. He's probably in the country by now. I didn't wait for him. I was so scared, Nicky," her voice broke off.

"I'm glad you came. Your guy is more help in this situation than mine would be, anyhow."

My guy? she thought, but for once, she didn't mind being teased by her little sister. Over the last week or so, she had regretted every time she'd yelled at her when they were growing up for stealing her clothes or makeup, every time she'd been mean to her, made fun of her. God, it was good to have her back again.

The rain was easing off. It stopped completely by the time they reached the water. The moon was out over the river, giving some visibility at last.

Brian was going for the boat. The water had lifted it while she'd been gone, but the rope had held.

One of the men came forward. "Where is the rest of the rescue team?"

She recognized his voice. He was the same guy who'd sparred with Brian before.

"This is it." Brian wrapped the rope around his arm and pulled the boat in, fought with the current. A couple of the other men went to help him.

"You gotta be kidding me. Is that the only boat?" The troublemaker was working up his righ-teous anger.

"Yep." Brian heaved.

"We won't all fit. I demand that my wife and I get on." He raised his rifle without pointing it at Brian, but making his meaning clear. "If anyone should stay behind it's you. Our taxes pay your salary."

She moved forward, knowing what was coming, but too late. The next second, the man was on his back in the mud, the rifle in Brian's hands.

"Take it easy, buddy." One of the men who was helping with the boat came over and spoke to the one on the ground. "He saved our lives. We need to thank him, shut up and do what he says."

The guy sat up, looking taken down a peg or two. He had wanted to take leadership of the group, probably. And he knew he wouldn't now. The rest wouldn't follow.

"Listen to me, all of you," Brian said. "There is a fair chance that we can all make it out of here, but it's not going to be easy. You are going to have to pull together. If you don't, you'll end up your own worst enemy. Two rules to remember—don't fight each other, don't fight the jungle."

He stepped back to the boat, tightened the rope.

Audrey moved over to him. "What are we going to do?"

He shook his head, and for the first time she saw something close to defeat in his eyes. And it scared her, more than anything had scared her so far.

"Not much until morning. Nobody can navigate this river in the dark. I was thinking about putting the weakest in the boat at first light. The rest of us can make it on foot." He shook his head.

"What's wrong with that plan?"

"Those who are too weak to walk, would

be too weak to handle the boat the way the river is now. And it's dangerous. Guerillas use the river. There are rap-ids. They would need me with them."

"Then go."

"The people in the forest need me, too. And even if I go with the boat, we'll have to stop to rest, to eat. We're not going to make it to civilization before August tenth."

Oh, God, there was still that. Some kind of attack, possibly thousands of lives at stake. She had for a while forgotten about it in the joy of having Nicky with her, safe.

"You should go alone, that would be fastest." Resolve filled her, as the idea blossomed in her mind. "We'll stay and you'll send help. You taught me enough so I should be able to keep everyone alive for a couple of days. We have weapons. You can help us get to a cave then leave."

She wished she felt a tenth of the self-confidence that she forced into her words. "Or you could take the strongest of the men with you," she added when she thought of the perils of the river.

He looked at her as if she'd just given him a million dollars, kissed her on the lips, just like that, in front of everyone, and strode to the group of hostages, but not to the biggest and tallest men. He went to the shortest one.

"How far is your tribe?"

"A day's walk down the hillside," the man responded in a lilting accent.

"How big is it?"

"About fifty men."

"Friendly with the guerillas?"

The man spat on the ground.

"Would they protect these people until I send help?"

"They don't have much, but they would share. It's the way of the jungle. We have fine witch doctor."

"Will you take them there?"

"I owe you my life. I do what you tell me."

Brian hesitated for a moment, then nodded. "Listen up," he addressed the others as the first light of dawn crept across the sky above them. "Your guide will take you to his village. It's one day of walking, everybody can manage that. I'm going down the river and will send help as soon as I can."

The man who had given him trouble lurched forward. "You're taking the boat and leaving us behind?"

But he couldn't rile Brian. He was perfectly calm now. "Which would you rather do? Walk for a day led by a man who grew up in the jungle and knows more than any of us about surviving in it? Or spend five days on a river that's flooding out of control and is controlled by guerillas, a plain target in a small boat where anyone with a gun can pick you off from shore?"

The man made some noise, but backed down.

"When do we leave?" another one asked.

"Now. If you run into the official Malaysian rescue team, or anyone at all with a radio, you have to let the authorities know that there is a credible terrorist threat for Kuala Lumpur for the tenth of August. Given where you spent the last week or so, they're going to believe you."

Another man stepped forward and shook Brian's hand, and then more came with their thanks and handshakes, wishing him speed down the river, some asking him to send word to family if he got the chance. Audrey wanted to move forward to do the same, but Nicky was hanging on to her hand just as tight as she could.

"Is this a good idea?"

"There just isn't an alternative." She hugged her, still getting used to them being together, that Nicky was alive, unharmed.

"When did you get to be so tough?" Nicky asked when they pulled away. "I thought I was the family daredevil."

"Oh yeah, and look where going on a jungle tour got you."

"When we get home I'll be sticking to kiddy parks with stroller trails."

"Exactly. Don't make me have to come after you again. You'll be an aunt soon. You're going to have to act responsible and dignified."

"Oh, man, you're kidding."

God, it was good to joke like that again. It made things feel a hell of a lot more normal, which they were still not. But the banter at least took some of the fright out of the night.

Brian sought her out at the end. "You'll

be all right. I'll have the army up here in no time."

"You must take someone with you. You need someone to watch your back." The sudden worry about him going alone seemed ridiculous. If anyone knew what they were doing it was him. He had a vast knowledge of jungle survival. And still, she hated to see him go.

"I doubt any of the men would want to leave their wives." He ran his hand down her arm in a gesture of farewell. "And they wouldn't be much help anyway. They don't know anything about the jungle. I'd be watching out for them."

"Take me then," she said, and pulled away from Nicky. "You can't go alone. I know the jungle. You taught me. You'll need help with the boat."

"Audrey, no." Nicky pulled her back. "This is crazy."

She turned and gave her sister a fierce hug. "He saved my life, and yours. I can't let him go alone."

Nicky hugged her tighter, but after a while nodded against her shoulder and let her go. She glanced from her to Brian. "Why do I think I'm missing something here? You two are not—"

"I'll be fine." Audrey cut her off.

"Take care of yourself," Nicky said with a bittersweet smile. "Take care of each other."

"Will do. And you, too."

"A walk in the park." Nicky picked up the rifle Brian had taken from the man with the big mouth, slung it over her shoulder and gave Audrey an if-you-can-do-it-so-can-I look, that was way too familiar.

She shook her head as she hugged her one more time, then she turned to Brian. "I'm ready."

"You are not coming," he said, his voice hard, his face serious.

Chapter Eight

How had this happened? Brian gripped the pole tight and, ignoring the rain, pushed a large chunk of driftwood away from the boat, looking ahead, while Audrey scanned the river and the jungle for dangers behind them.

She was one determined woman. But to be truthful, he'd rather have her watch his back than anyone else. She was tough, had learned over the last couple of days not to be squeamish, and pulled her own weight. And he knew her at least a little, more so than any of the men among the hostages. She had earned his trust.

They were on the way back. He felt lighter with the first half of their mission done. The hostages were reasonably safe. They had a good guide and good weapons.

"Do you think they'll reach the village safely?" Audrey asked, her mind obviously running along the same lines as his.

"They should be fine. Hamid's men are probably nursing their injuries, holed up somewhere. If they think the army is in this part of the jungle, they are probably trying to hide."

"What does he want anyway? Him and Omar and the rest?"

He shrugged. "What do opposition forces always want? A change in government."

"To overthrow the monarchy?"

"Not quite. From what I heard over the years, Hamid figures himself to be some kind of a tragically overlooked heir to the throne. You should see the tattoo on his arm, a leaping tiger from wrist to elbow with a crown on his head."

"Kidnapping people—there's a real prince."

"He's raising money for a coup. And if he scares some foreigners out of the country at the same time, that's fine with him, too. He's a religious extremist."

"And Omar?"

"I don't think he much believes in their cause, and he doesn't follow any religion, that's for sure. He likes fighting. He wants power and since he doesn't have any under this government, he figures he might have better luck with the next, especially if he helps to bring it about."

He pushed some debris away from the boat, a bunch of branches and the bloated body of a young wild pig tangled up between them. He registered a moment of regret that the meat was too far gone to eat.

"They're halfway there," she said, and he knew she was thinking about Nicky.

"I can't believe you left your sister for me."

"I'm a known masochist. A glutton for punishment," she said in a dry voice.

"I thought maybe some kind of jungle fever addled your reasoning."

She turned a little, one perfect eyebrow cocked. "Ever considered you might be able to get more from a girl by sweet-talk-ing than by calling her a lunatic?"

And his breath caught, as if someone had dropped a boulder on his chest. Be-cause their conversation was so normal, so lighthearted, so not something he'd ex-pected. It was almost as if she were flirting with him, sounding as if she wouldn't have minded at all if he tried to sweet-talk her.

God almighty. Did he still know how to sweet-talk? He felt like he just came across a field of landmines. And acting appropri-ately, he backed away.

"Your sister will be fine." He slid from the seat and sat on the bottom of the boat, ignoring the few inches of water. "Pull your head in. We're close to camp."

Audrey ducked down beneath the branches that covered the boat on the side and on top, making it look like a tangled mass of a tree trunk broken off by the storm, floating downriver. They were in the middle of the water, letting the current carry them.

"Do you think they're watching the river?" She breathed the words.

"Not for us at this stage. We've been

gone too long. But for flooding maybe. Omar's camp is not that far from here."

"But if the guerillas who ran off into the jungle last night got here before us—" she whispered.

"The boat is going a lot faster than anyone can in the jungle. Some will come to Omar without a doubt, but by the time they get here, we'll be far downriver."

He held his head up enough to see through the branches, keeping an eye out for driftwood, listening for anything suspicious, be it man-made noise or the sound of rapids ahead. He kept as low as he could. Their disguise was good enough to fool someone who happened to catch a glimpse of them from the corner of his eye, but would not stand up to closer scrutiny.

They cleared the area where Omar's men would have been if they were out there, but were slowed down shortly after that, coming to a stretch where the river widened out. The surface was littered with debris the water had washed down from the mountains. Audrey directed the boat, while he used his pole to keep anything large from crashing into them—hard work for both of them. Night approached by the time they fought their way through the rough spot.

They pulled the boat to shore, up on higher ground as far in as they could, and turned it upside down to keep the rain from filling it, covered it with fallen leaves and branches.

"It's not bad from afar." Audrey stood back when they were done. "As long as nobody comes too close."

"There's less than an hour left before nightfall. Let's hope our luck holds." He moved forward.

"I'm starving," she blurted out. "Sorry, didn't mean to complain. Nothing you can do about it."

While their progress on the river was much faster than it would have been on land, it had disadvan-tages. Not being able to forage for food was one of them. He searched the trees above for any sign of fruit as they went. "We'll find something."

No time to fish now. He had to find a place to spend the night, light a fire, build a shelter. All that before darkness fell. But luck was with them for once—they came across a rock formation not a hundred feet from the river. There was a large indentation in the rock, not quite a cave, but a ledge that would protect them from the elements.

"Up there." He pointed, and helped Audrey climb.

Looked like they weren't the first to discover the place. Ashes blackened the rock floor farther in, leftovers of a long-ago fire. There were piles of leaves the wind had blown into the back of the crevice, a couple of chunks of deadwood left behind by whoever had that fire. Enough to start one now.

"Here." He handed Audrey the waterproof matches he'd grabbed at the guerilla camp, then pulled the papers from his shirt. "Try to dry these."

He hadn't had a chance to look at them yet, didn't want to get them any wetter than he had to.

"I'm gonna look for some food." He stepped back out into the rain that had turned into a downpour.

He didn't bother to look for grubs, there

was no sense searching the muddy ground. He walked back toward the river and looked for palm trees, came across a patch of wild berries and settled for that, picked his shirt full of the small semi-soft fruit. They'd had a poor diet so far, one that they couldn't make it on in the long term, but sufficient to get them through the next couple of days.

He spotted something high up a tree, thought it might be fruit, climbed and found it to be orchids, a multitude of them, and on a whim, he filled the rest of the room in his shirt with blossoms.

AUDREY LAID the mess of soaked papers near the fire next to her clothes, close enough to dry fast, but not so close that they'd burn. She anchored them with a stone to make sure a gust of wind didn't blow them into harm's way.

"Anything useful on them?" Brian climbed up and sat next to her, dripped on the floor. He took off his hat and wiped the water off his face, brushed his hair back.

"Too soggy. Didn't think I could pull

them all apart without tearing them. Probably better to wait until they dry."

He looked over the ones that were readable. Blueprints one after the other, but no writing on them, no identification of what building they belonged to. Only one of the sheets was different. It contained some kind of a scribbled list.

"Embassies." Brian picked up that one. "That's something. If we get to KL in time, this might be enough of a clue to head off tragedy." He set the sheet down and placed a stone on top carefully, before turning back to her.

She eyed his bulging shirtfront with hope. "Find anything?"

He looked embarrassed for a second, reluctant.

"What?"

He reached inside and scooped a giant handful of white-pink blossoms, then hesitantly laid them at her bare feet.

"Oh, my God, these are beautiful." She glanced up at him. "Are they edible?"

He laughed, the first real laugh she'd heard from him, and it reached to her heart.

He scooped out another handful, then another. The light of the fire danced on the petals, a soft scent filling their small shelter.

"They are for you," he said. "For coming with me."

She stared at him, speechless, the gesture so sweet and unexpected she didn't know for a moment how to react. "Thank you," she said, and although she wanted to reach out to him, she didn't. He hadn't reacted well to that in the past.

But there was something in the orchid-scented air between them that hadn't been there before. It made her feel self-conscious of the fact that she wore nothing but her underwear and tanktop, even though it had not been the first time she'd taken off her clothes to dry, nor was it the least amount of clothes he'd seen her in.

"These are to eat." He brought forth handfuls of berries next, and she fell on them shamelessly.

When his shirt was empty, he took it off and laid it by the fire to dry, putting his pants next to it. She kept her gaze averted as she ate. There was a newfound awareness between them, she didn't know what to do with. At some point he had transformed from wild man to simply a man she was interested in. It was absolutely crazy. They knew nothing about each other.

"Where did you grow up?"

"Ladder, a very small town. My father worked for the post office. My mother was a homemaker."

She deleted the cowboy image she'd been trying to put together. It never quite gelled anyway. "You never told me your full name."

He held her gaze, his masculine lips stretching into a wry smile. "Old habits die hard. I don't suppose it matters now. Brian Welkins."

He'd been on some secret jungle mission before he'd gotten captured. She didn't ask more about that. But she did want to know more about him. She knew his parents were gone and that he'd been their only child, adopted.

"Are you married?" she asked as it suddenly occurred to her, her heart beating harder as she waited for his response.

"Come on now, you've known me long enough to know that no woman would be crazy enough to have me." He was joking, but there was a sour tone to his words.

"You're not missing much. Marriage isn't all it's cracked up to be."

"Can't say I've ever been tempted to give it a try."

She stirred the fire with a stick. If they could keep it going for a while longer, they would have dry clothes for sleeping.

"My parents got divorced when I was in high school. I was so mad at them. I wanted a real family again. I got married way too early, for all the wrong reasons. Even if we didn't have all that stress from not being able to have a baby, I doubt we would have lasted. We just would have floundered longer."

Silence stretched between them.

"The bugs got you." He reached out to trace a finger over the row of red bumps on her arm.

The blinding lust that hit her out of nowhere froze her limbs for a moment, knocked the air out of her lungs. He misunderstood her reaction and pulled away.

"It's okay," she said, then felt embarrassed.

It's okay? What was she, an idiot?

His blue gaze fastened on her face. "I don't want you to be afraid of me. I would never hurt you."

"I'm not afraid." She ran her own finger over the tingling line his left behind. "I just don't always know what to expect."

He nodded and gave her a rueful smile. "Me neither." He looked away. "I'm not like other people. I've been away too long. I want to be just a man, but I don't know if I can do it."

There was a tug in the vicinity of her heart. "You are everything any man could ever hope to be. You're a hero," she said when she recovered.

"I'm damaged. And I want things I cannot have."

From the way he was looking at her, she understood what he wanted, and her blood lurched into a sprint through her veins.

What do I want? She looked away and her gaze fell on the orchids at her feet. *Him.* She wanted him, scars and all.

He stretched out on his back, his hands folded behind his head, his eyes closed. She scooted over and lay next to him on her side, watched the rise and fall of his chest in the light of the fire. Even undernourished, he was the most physically perfect man she had known. The scars that marred his skin could not detect from the strength of his body, the beauty of the muscles that carried her up the trees and pulled her out of the river.

She touched a fingertip to a raised bump. "The bugs got you, too." Her finger glided on to the next and the one beyond that, zig-zagging over his ribcage.

He placed a hand over hers, pressed her palm against his skin. His heartbeat raced as fast as hers did. She looked up and found his eyes open, his gaze heated. And then she was scared. Not of him, but of her own reaction. Because she wanted him, a stranger, more than she had ever wanted another man before, more than she had wanted her husband.

She looked away, only to be confronted with the proof of his desire under the stretching loincloth.

"Brian…" Her voice tripped.

"Let me touch you." He waited, giving her time to say no.

Instead, she closed her eyes.

She expected an intimate caress, his fingers circling her breasts, or outlining her aching nipples. But it was the back of his hand on her cheek that she felt. And when his fingers did come to play on her skin, he drew with them the line of her jaw, her eyes, her lips. He followed the curve of her neck, hesitated at the hollow spot there and replaced his fingers with his lips and tasted her. And when he pulled away, she opened her eyes and looked into his.

"You're seducing me," she said, feeling as if the heat of the fire had moved deep inside her.

"I would love that more than anything." His sexy lips stretched into a semblance of a smile. "If I still knew how."

"Hey." She grinned at him. "I might not be as experienced as the average teenager, but I still know when I'm being seduced."

He dipped his head to the valley between her breasts, until she could feel his hot breath through the thin material of the tanktop. "I'll let you be the judge of things then," he said.

He pressed his lips to her body, dragged them over her breast until his mouth was over a nipple, then he sucked it through the tanktop. She grew damp between her legs in response and arched her back, shameless, wanting all he was willing to give.

His fingers moved over her stomach and gripped her hips and he ground himself into her. The shock of it, the electricity that zinged through her, brought her to the edge. It was too much, too soon. She wasn't used to it. Her body didn't work at these speeds.

He pulled back and scooped up the flowers, held them above her then let them slip through his fingers one by one, raining white-pink blossoms over her body. He kept one, feathered the soft petals over her lips, her neck, across the narrow strip of skin that showed between her tanktop and panties, then moved lower and caressed the soles of her feet, drawing curlicues with the orchid up her inner thighs.

When he got where he was headed, he brushed the flower over her underwear a couple of times before tucking it into the band. She trembled as he pressed his hot palm against her.

In a circular motion he pushed and massaged, while he bent over and fastened his lips on her nipple, her clothes still between them. He changed the rhythm then, to slower strokes, up and down, then circular again, the heel of his palm against her opening, his fingers against her swollen nub of pleasure.

As he had pulled her up hillsides, and rocks and trees to save her life, he pulled her now to the sky, higher and higher. And then his teeth closed over her nipple and she tumbled.

The first thing she could hear was her own harsh breathing, her body still contracting. She looked at his badly cut hair, his head resting between her breasts, her mind swimming in confusion as her body was still swimming in bliss. How could he so fast? What he had done to her? Was it even possible?

She still had her clothes on, he'd never even gotten as far as her naked skin, let alone having any part of him inside her. Sweet heavens. The man and the way her body had responded to him took her by surprise. He singed her, turned her inside out. She loved every second of it. Audrey reached for him and ran her fingers through his hair, caressed his back.

He pulled up and turned her with her back to him, locked her tight into his arms. His lips were pressed hot against her shoulder, but he didn't move them, didn't move anything, although she could feel his hard length against her bottom. There was a thrill in knowing that she affected him this way.

"Go to sleep," he whispered into her ear, brushing his warm lips over her lobe.

"Brian?" She tried to turn and found herself gent-ly restrained. "You don't have to— I mean, I want to. I want you."

Lord, it sounded pitiful and shameless. Her body hadn't even fully calmed down yet, but she did want him, again, still. How could he not know that? Or was there more to it?

He had broken through all her defenses with amazing speed and ease. And now she realized he wasn't about to let her come anywhere near his. The mask was still firmly in place. Was he hiding from her, or from himself?

He pressed his lips to her skin again, then repeated, "Go to sleep."

And from the strain in his voice she understood what it cost him to rein in his own passion.

"Let me touch you, then."

He drew a deep breath. "Maybe another time."

"Tomorrow we might not be alive. You need me as much as I need you."

"I don't want you to give yourself to me because I need you. Not to escape from reality, not for pity."

"Pity has nothing to do with it." The fierce denial tumbled from her lips. She tried to turn again, frustrated by the arms that wouldn't let her. "It's not fair. It's not fair to either of us."

She could feel his heartbeat against her back, slow and measured. Hers, on the other hand, was still scrambling. His heat enveloped her, comforted her, and it made her mad that he wouldn't let her give the same comfort to him. "What reason would you accept? What do you want?"

He touched his forehead against the back of her head and stayed silent for so long, she didn't think he would respond at all.

"I don't know," he whispered, his voice raspy and full of emotion. "I no longer even know who I am."

THE ARMY was in the jungle.

Hamid leaned his back against the rough stone of the cave, trying to think through the throbbing pain in his shoulder. At least it was cool in here, although far from quiet. His men in the back made plenty of noise, arguing about the attack the night before and taking care of their injuries, cursing the Royal Malaysian troops.

For a moment back at the tin mine, he had been certain the negotiator was bluffing. But no, his own men came across a village messenger this morning. There were soldiers not ten miles to the east of here.

They could be the ones who had attacked his camp, returning now with the hostages. He should have been notified when they'd first entered the jungle. Anger pulsed through him. Where had the village watchers been then? An example would have to be made. But not yet. He had other things to take care of first.

"I have an important job for you," he told the man across the fire from him.

"Anything," Omar responded.

A spark flew from the fire and landed by his feet, going out quickly on the cold stone.

"You must gather your men and what's left of mine and attack the army. We must slow them down, cause a distraction." Enough of a distraction for him to slip unseen down the river. He had to get to a doctor—there was one near Miri he trusted, one who had helped him in the past. Then he had to get to KL in time.

The fire popped, its flames not substantial enough to light the whole cave, but enough to show the greed on Omar's face. He missed Jamil, even if they hadn't always agreed on everything.

"I will defeat this army unit, I will take their big guns, I will unite the camps. And when you give the signal from KL, I'll be ready." The younger man punctuated his words by bringing his fist down on his knee.

Hamid sat straight, wanting to press his palm against the pain in his shoulder, but resisting. It would not be smart to show any sign of weakness in front of Omar.

"You are instrumental to the success of our cause," he said, and watched the calculating look in the other man's eyes.

He would have to be taken care of before he became a problem. But not yet. He still had usefulness left in him. And things were bad enough so they couldn't be picky.

He would let Omar handle the army unit. If the young hothead won, it would be a victory for them all. If he lost, and something happened to him…one less problem to worry about.

The camps were more or less united, and once he succeeded in KL, the stragglers would accept his leadership. But he had problems aplenty in other areas. Having the hostages escape had dealt a blow to phase two of his plan. He had counted on the ransom money for more weapons, had a couple of surface-to-air missiles on order. He needed them to effectively fight the Royal Air Force. He needed a decisive military victory.

"Stop by Ali's camp once you cross the river," he said, on second thought. "He will join you if you tell him I sent you."

"I don't need Ali."

"You misunderstand me, friend. It is Ali who needs you. I fear your brother was trying to convince him that a major offensive was not necessary. It would be good for him to see the army, to realize they were already in the forest. It would help him understand that the war has already started, whether he wanted it or not."

He needed Ali's calm reason to temper Omar's blind courage. They both would hate working with the other, but they would make a stronger team than either one fighting alone.

Allah willing, his line would be restored to the throne soon, the country put into the service of the one true god instead of foreign business interests. It had been bad enough when the Chinese skimmed off profits, and most businesses were owned by them, while the Malay people worked the land, peasants and servants in their own country. But at least the Chinese who lived on the peninsula had kept the profits invested in the country. They kept to themselves and respected Muslim law even if they didn't practice it.

The Western influx of businesses was changing the face of the country, however, and the government welcomed the Europeans and Americans, who looked at the natives as barbarians to be exploited. In its mindless quest for modernization, the government failed to protect the culture of the country and its citizens. Young Malay people worked in sweatshops under conditions little better than slavery, making products they would never be able to afford to buy, for business owners who took the profits and distributed them to their shareholders back in the west.

His country was under occupation, not by a foreign army, but by foreign businessmen. And to make things worse, it was the country's very own government who held it down, allowing it to be raped.

He was fighting in a righteous war. And he couldn't lose. If he lived to see victory, he would be king. If he fell, he'd be a martyr for his cause, and his brother would be forced to give up his misguided acceptance of the status quo. Yes, his brother would be forced to avenge him, to take up his weapons.

Either way, the true line of succession would be restored soon. The KL attack would start a tide that could not be turned back.

Chapter Nine

Brian listened to the night, feeling every breath Audrey took, every heartbeat. She might not have thought that was enough for him, but in the past few years there had been plenty of times when he had thought he would never have another moment like this.

She had seen where he'd been, what he'd become, and yet she accepted him. He was stunned and humbled at once. He wanted to get up, rush out into the rain and dance, twirl her around, or bang his chest and shout into the night like Tarzan in triumph. Since she was sleeping, she probably wouldn't have appreciated either display of joy.

He stared into the darkness, trying to get his mind around all that had happened in the last couple of days, all the ways his life had changed. He sure hadn't foreseen this when he'd planned his escape.

He was laying amidst flower petals, with a beautiful woman in his arms.

It wasn't the first time—he had once known how to woo. But it was the most significant, the one he would never forget. And not because of the extraordinary circumstances, but because of the extraordinary woman.

He relaxed his arms, realizing suddenly how tense his muscles were. Something prickled his instincts, and he turned his attention to the outside world. He lifted his head and listened, but couldn't hear much over the rain. Their fire had gone out long ago. He reached for their clothes, finally dry.

"Audrey," he whispered to her. "Wake up. We have to get dressed."

She came awake at once. "What's wrong?"

He wasn't sure. There was now a slight tremor in the rock beneath them. Something popped in the distance, then again and again. Not gunfire. He yanked on his pants and shirt, his boots, found the papers and tucked them away. "Where are the matches?"

"In my pocket."

The sounds were getting louder. A rumble, like logs rolling. Had the river risen this high? Couldn't be. Not overnight. And then it clicked.

"Mudslide!" He grabbed her and they half slid, half fell off the rock. "This way. Away from the river."

The natural slope of the land would give the mud direction. He didn't want to get caught in its path. He couldn't see it, could barely see a foot in front of his nose, but he knew the monster behind him. He'd seen it kill before in Haiti. He'd been part of the marine rescue crew that had retrieved the bodies. Mudslides were ferocious killers.

They ran, giving everything to it, but it soon became apparent they couldn't outrun the force of nature. Not in the dark, not with his bad knee. He searched for the biggest tree around, and prayed they were out of the main flow.

"Grab on." He latched on to a handful of vines and climbed up the tree with Audrey on his back.

"Is it safe up here?" she asked when they were sitting in the V of a branch.

"Safer than down there. Unless the mud takes the tree."

And as if to underscore his words, the monster reached them, shaking their precarious haven. He could hear trees falling all around, but theirs held. And then a thunderous crack rent the air and their branch shook as if a giant whacked his axe into the tree.

"What was that?"

"Probably a log hitting us." The mud rolled everything in its path with it.

"Will it knock down the tree?"

"Not a log, no."

"But?"

"A rolling boulder could. We should be out of the main flow though." He put his arm around her to make sure she didn't fall should the tree get hit again and shake harder.

She clung to him. He was aware of every point where they touched. Her soft body seemed to melt into his. He ran his hand down her back in a gesture of comfort, and found himself comforted by her nearness.

The rain was still coming down pretty hard, the few minutes they had actually spent in dry clothes nothing but a distant memory. When she shivered, he held her tighter, offering her some of his own body heat. "It'll be better when the sun comes up."

"It's fine," she said. "We're going to make it. We're both too stubborn to die."

He grinned into the darkness, his arms woven around her. They waited for sunrise like that, sleep impossible under the circumstances.

The devastation around them became apparent as soon as the first light of dawn appeared on the sky. That they could see the sky, was a telltale sign in itself. The thick canopy was gone; the trees razed where the main flow had been, thinned considerably on the edge. Their tree was one of the few still standing. The mud covered everything below.

"How deep do you think it is?"

He looked at the trees that had survived the night. "A couple of feet."

"Can we walk in it?"

He nodded. "But it would take us too long to fight our way to dry ground. And it's still raining. The mud might start moving again." He stepped over to another branch so he could see all around.

"Are we trapped?"

He grabbed a thick vine, tested it with his weight. "Ready to go?"

She was staring at him wide-eyed. "You can't be serious."

"You wrap it around one foot like this, hang on tight, and push away with the other. I'll be right there to catch you." He swung as hard as he could, sailed through the air, latching on to a branch on the next standing tree. "Come on, there's nothing to it." He threw the vine back.

She hesitated.

"I'm going to catch you. You have to trust me," he called out to her.

But his heart lurched into his throat when she did kick away and flew for a few precarious moments in the air, until he finally grabbed on to her and crushed her to him.

She looked up at him with a smile. "It wasn't too bad."

A couple of seconds passed before every nerve ending in his body got the message that she was here, safe in his arms, and he could let her go.

"Glad you feel that way," he said, "because we're going to have to do this again."

The second swing took them clear of the mud that now cut them off from the river.

"We can't get to the boat, can we?"

"Even if we could make it over there, I doubt we would find it."

"So we'll walk?"

"For now." They didn't have another option. "Walking would get us out of the jungle eventually, but it won't get us to civilization in time to warn Kuala Lumpur of the attack."

"We have to get back to the water."

"As soon as we can."

He started out, following the edge of the mudslide toward the river, and they walked all morning until they finally reached the

Baram around noontime. It was tamer than he'd expected.

"The mud might have dammed it up somewhere above us. I wouldn't want to be on the water when that dam breaks," he said. Not that that was a worry at this stage. They no longer had a boat.

"Look over there." Audrey pointed to a fallen log down the bank.

The vegetation had been flattened by water that had overflowed the river basin not long ago, debris littering the muddy bank. He scanned the thick chunk of wood that had caught her attention.

Not just a log. He scrutinized the pointed end as he walked toward it. A canoe. The water must have lifted it somewhere up-river and dumped it down here. He ran, praying it wasn't broken, that half of it wasn't missing but was just buried in the mud. He was digging around it by the time Audrey caught up with him.

"Give me a hand. Pull here."

They heaved it toward the water and he flipped it over, scooped out the mud that still remained inside. As far as canoes went, it was a rather primitive one, cut with an axe from one piece of wood. And no paddles, he felt around in the mud, coming up empty-handed.

He grabbed a flat, straight piece of driftwood—better than nothing—then with Audrey's help pushed the canoe in the water. It didn't sink. *So far, so good.*

"Get in."

When she did, he handed her the rifles then pushed the canoe out far enough so the current would catch and carry it. But before he could climb up next to her, the canoe caught on something and rolled, taking her under.

She didn't come up.

He could see nothing in the murky water, tried to feel around with one hand while holding the canoe with the other. He couldn't let the water take that. They needed it. Had Audrey hit her head? Had she gotten tangled in something?

He plunged under, searched desperately while struggling to keep the canoe in place. Oh, hell. He let go and clawed the opaque water with both hands, mad panic gripping him. How long had she been under? Less than a minute, it couldn't have been a full minute yet, although it felt like a lifetime.

Then his fingers brushed against cloth and he grabbed on, pulled her up. She was limp in his arms. He shook her and when he did, she sputtered and opened her eyes, pressed a hand against the reddish bump on her forehead.

"Can you stand?"

She nodded, coughing hard, and steadied herself.

The rifles. No time to look for them now. He threw himself into the water and went after the canoe. Damn, the current was strong. He caught the thing at last, afloat still with the air trapped under it. He struggled to turn it over and managed somehow, holding it in place with one hand, bailing water out with the other. There was no way he could drag it the fifty feet up to where she stood.

And she must have understood it, because she began walking, then swimming toward him. And after an eternity she reached him at last, and he heaved her into the canoe and got in after her.

"You're okay," he said instead of asking, not to reassure her, but because he needed to hear it, then went back to scooping water.

She pitched in, her hands shaky. They didn't stop until they were down to the last couple of finger's width in the bottom. The rain was easing off, the sun making a half-hearted effort to break through the clouds.

"How bad are you hurt?"

She tried to smile, but failed miserably. "Nicky used to get me worse while playing tennis."

"Runaway ball?"

"Runaway racket." She coughed. "We used to play doubles. She's like a windmill. A serious hazard on the court." The words were said with obvious love.

He brushed her wet hair out of her face. They'd both lost their hats—the least of his worries at the moment.

"I have a hard time picturing you in an ordinary life, playing tennis. I've only seen you as part of the jungle. An Amazon."

She laughed, but it turned into a coughing fit. He didn't dare reach out and pull her to him, for fear that they would upset the canoe's balance again.

"What are we going to do?" she asked when she could talk.

"We're fine for now."

The water carried them straight down the middle, but sooner or later he would need something to steer them away from drifting logs and other hazards. The river floated enough broken branches to make a pole or even another makeshift paddle, he just had to wait until they got close enough to one to grab it.

Audrey coughed the last of the water out of her lungs. "Phew. That was nasty. I'm not doing that again."

The thought that he could have lost her squeezed his lungs until he was breathing as hard as she was.

"You keep saving my life." Her jungle-green eyes looked at him, endless wells of trust.

He leaned forward carefully, cupped her face, and with his thumbs brushed off the drops of water that clung to her eyelashes.

"Maybe it's *you* who is saving *my* life," he said, and kissed her.

And got lost in the softness of her lips. He had denied himself this the night before, and he had been right to do so. Because now that he reached the gates of heaven, there was no going back.

The meeting of their lips was like kissing for the first time—tentative, excitement mixing with a sense of awe. His hands moved to her shoulders to gather her closer, and she pressed against him. Then the canoe rocked and it brought him back to reason fast and hard.

He straightened and looked around, pushed away the jumble of driftwood that had bumped into them, keeping a sturdy stick that looked long enough to be of some help. Only when their path was clear did he turn his attention back to her, painfully aware that the slightest distraction, the smallest error in judgment could cost both of them their lives. What the hell had he been thinking?

That he wanted her more than he had ever wanted anything.

But he couldn't have her. Not under these circumstances, perhaps not ever.

"Keep your eye on the back, I'll watch the front. Same as we did with the boat."

And as they soon came to a spot where a tributary came into the river, making navigation even harder, that was the last piece of conversation they had for the rest of the day, other than quick directions thrown at each other.

When night fell they pulled the canoe out of the water and dragged it with them inland, not wanting to lose it. It was smaller and lighter than the boat.

He made their shelter far enough in the forest so that even if the water rose it wouldn't reach them—a makeshift platform, and two poles at each end that held the canoe upside down above them like a roof. They dined on a handful of crunchy roots he'd dug up by the riverbank. Then, unable to light a fire without smoking themselves out, they snuggled together for sleep.

A part of him, the selfish part, wished they would never find their way out of the jungle.

She lay facing him, his arms around her. The rain that had started up again drowned out everything but the sound of their breathing. She brought her hand up to his face.

"You are..." She took a deep breath. "You are not like anyone I've ever known."

He wasn't, although he would have given anything to be just an average man, someone who could have hoped for a future that included the woman in his arms. The darkness that surrounded them seeped into his heart.

"Are you telling me that I'm rough around the edges?" He tried to make light of it, and wished he could see her face, read her thoughts in her eyes. He could barely make out the shape of her head.

"Complex," she said. "On the one hand, you can kill a man without blinking an eye, which scares the crap out of me." She hesitated. "On the other hand, you are thoughtful, and gentle, and protective, and I have never felt as safe as I do when I'm with you."

His heart beat a slow thumping rhythm.

He saw himself differently. He was like the jungle—too overgrown, impossible to clear. His past was a tangle of vines that bound him.

She stretched up to put her lips against his.

Their soft comfort caught him by surprise. And he took them, because his throat suddenly tight, speech was beyond his ability. He felt as if in a fantasy, as if kissing a dream.

He brushed his lips across hers tentatively, knowing it would be better to leave things at that, but he couldn't. He covered her mouth with kisses from corner to corner, outlining the soft arches that drove him mad during the day. Then he kissed her face, wanting to drink her beauty until it replaced the darkness inside him. He pressed his lips against each eyelid in turn, grateful and humbled that she saw beyond appearances and somehow managed to glimpse the last vestiges of the man he had once been.

When he was done covering her with kisses, he returned to her mouth again. She parted her lips for him, and his heart melted. She tasted mildly spicy, like the roots they had eaten for dinner, intoxicating. He deepened the kiss, lost in the moment, lost in the sweetness of her.

"Audrey," he whispered her name when they came up briefly for air.

She slid her hands under his shirt, and desire washed through his body, the sensation so hot and hard it took his breath away all over again. A mudslide couldn't have buried him so completely.

He didn't dare move while she unbuttoned his shirt, fearing he would scare her away, still expecting her to change her mind, to stop. It would have been probably the sanest thing to do.

But she didn't, not even when her fingers glided over his scars.

He reached for the bottom of her shirt, hesitant, but she helped him, and with the T-shirt and tanktop as well. And then her bare skin was against his, a sensation so overwhelming that for a moment he didn't move, just held on to her, memorizing it. The gentle curve of her breasts pressed against him, and when she shifted and her nipples dragged across his skin, a groan rumbled up his throat.

He waited for the mad, animal-like need that he had feared he would not be able to control, but instead he found another emotion surge from deep inside, one that didn't have to do as much with the primal act of sex as with this one specific woman.

His body had needs, yes, and they'd gone long unsatisfied, but he didn't just want to take her body. He needed more than release. He wanted to make love to her. He lifted his lips from hers and buried his head in the crook of her neck for a long moment, soaking up the exquisite sensation of their bodies touching.

His hands sought her soft skin, the curves he wanted to get lost in forever. He drank from her lips again, and unwrapped the rest of her as carefully as a child unwraps a most treasured present.

"You're beautiful," he said, and heard her chuckle in response.

"That compliment loses some of its effectiveness in the pitch-dark night."

"I have you memorized. And I don't need light to know the beauty in here." He put his palm over her heart.

She pressed her lips to his in response. The kiss was slow but thorough. When she tugged on his pants, he turned to make it easier, but resisted to help, to rush. The feel of her hands on him, there, sent fire coursing through his veins.

They finally had nothing between them, and he gently turned her on her back and tasted her at his leisure, her lips, the hollow of her neck, her breasts. He skimmed his fingers over her flat belly, drawing circles around her belly button, playing games over the curve of her hip.

He wanted to discover every inch of her, taste every patch of skin, make it his if only for a night.

He moved lower and tangled his fingers in the silky curls between her thighs, drew a fingertip over the parting line slowly, inch by inch, from one end to the other, then made the trail back up again.

"Oh," she said, breathless, when he slipped into her. Her breasts pushed into his chest as she arched against him.

The way she responded to his touch was a wonder. She opened to him, gave herself to him freely and with abandon.

Nearly blind with need, he moved deeper

inside, with one finger first, then two, and felt her respond, but then she reached for his wrist and pulled his hand away.

He obeyed, his ears ringing with the harshness of his breathing, willing his heated desire to calm, even as his body screamed for her. He wouldn't push her. If this was as far as she was willing to go, so be it. If it killed him, this was it.

But instead of pulling away, she pressed the palm of her other hand to his hardness and folded her fingers around him. "I want all of you."

Her words seared across his skin, sending every drop of blood he had into the part she was holding.

He pushed against her, pumped his hip—he couldn't help it now. She brought her hands to the small of his back, parted her legs and lifted her knees. He ran his fingers across her inner thighs. When she moaned with impatience, he moved over her, slipped one hand under her firm buttocks and lifted her for his entry.

"Are you sure?" He could barely croak the words out.

"Yes!" She leaned up and bit his shoulder, slipped her hands over his buttocks. "Trust me, I'm not going to get pregnant. And otherwise, I'm as healthy as a woman can get. I've been tested to oblivion during the fertility treatments."

He had been, too, he wanted to reassure her. Regular checkups for the members of the SDDU were mandatory and exhausting. Then she did some wicked little movement with her hips, rendering him unable to speak, managing no more than a reassuring grunt.

Her opening was moist and tight, and for a moment he simply rested against it, trying to catch his breath—a futile effort. He outlined her perineum with his dewy tip. She responded by squeezing her long slim fingers into his buttocks. *Oh, man.*

He pushed in a slow inch, then backed out, moved forward again. Her glorious body stretched to allow him in.

"Brian…" Like a prayer, she whispered his name.

Next time we make love I want to see your face, the thought burned through his mind, rushing to his lips. But since they both knew there wouldn't be a next time, he kept his mouth shut and lost himself in her.

The world fell away as he pumped in and out and, answering his rhythm, she moved beneath him. He dipped to taste her mouth, plundering her at the same time below and above, then moved to her breasts and ravaged them one after the other, his control slipping now.

He wanted to consume her, as she was consuming him, burning him up with need.

He wanted to race to heaven with her, and at the same time, he struggled desperately to hold back, to make it last forever.

He felt her body grip him even tighter, squeeze him with quick contractions, milking him wave after wave. There was no holding back then. He poured into her with so much force, it felt like he was pouring his soul out.

Bliss. Floating. Eternity.

Neither of them could move or talk for some time.

Then in some hazy recess of his mind a thought arose that he must be crushing her, so he flipped them over, sprawling her on top.

They stayed like that forever.

"That was hot," she said next to his ear, still gasping for air.

He grinned weakly into the night. "If it wasn't raining, we would have started a forest fire."

She giggled. An honest-to-goodness giggle. And it made something leap deep inside his heart.

He held her closer, tighter.

"What?"

"Nothing. I wish I could see you. I want to make sure you're real, not just a trick from some jungle spirit."

She took his hand and put it over her madly beating heart. "It's real," she said.

He kissed her, feeling her heart in the palm of his hand, and refused to think of that other reality that waited for them outside the jungle.

HER BONES were made of rubber, and just the memory of last night was enough to set her body tingling. Audrey stirred, opened her eyes and found Brian still sleeping. The rise and fall of his chest was slow and even. She spread her fingers on the middle of his chest where her hand rested, skimming the hard muscles beneath her fingertips.

He had made love to her with such gentleness, such reverence. He had been right. It did feel unreal. If they weren't still naked, entangled in each other, she would have thought it a dream. She burrowed into him, emotion choking her all of a sudden.

Last night had been the most beautiful night of her life. They'd had no champagne, no candles, no chocolate, not even a real bed—nothing normally associated with romance and seduction.

But none of it mattered, the magic had come from between them.

She let her gaze glide over the awakening forest, drinking in the peaceful beauty of it. Frogs were singing a serenade. The rain had stopped, she realized just as Brian's arm tightened around her. She glanced up at him. He was awake after all, but was keeping his eyes at a slit.

"Somebody's watching us," he whispered, his lips barely moving.

Fear replaced her good mood in an instant, and she turned into him more to hide her nakedness. The guerillas had caught up with them. For a moment she panicked, then from somewhere deep welled up new-found strength and resolve.

Screw them. She was ready to fight. For herself and Brian, for what they had found last night. Nobody was going to take that away from her.

"Is your knife within reach?" He slid his hand off her, maneuvering closer to his own weapon.

"I lost it when I lost the boat."

She heard something move in the bushes ahead to the left, lifted a little so if Brian had to jump up, he could get his arm from under her neck with ease.

But instead, he suddenly relaxed, letting his head fall back with a strangled laugh.

"What?"

"Look." He nodded toward the forest, and a second later a large orangutan sashayed out into the open.

He stopped and looked them over with interest, his orange fur wet and matted. The open perusal on his face was nearly human. She felt embarrassed by her nakedness.

Oh dear. She looked for her pants—out of reach.

Brian got up and pulled on his clothes. She stayed where she was, staring at the animal, too scared to move. It was pretty big, as tall as four feet, showing some nasty teeth as it curled its black lips.

"Is it dangerous?"

"Nah. Harmless things."

The orangutan lumbered closer, fingered the platform she was lying on, poked her naked belly. She forced herself to stay still, not wanting to provoke it. She was a city girl. She didn't know how to deal with wild animals. Her only exposure to the animal kingdom had been a couple of goldfish back in grade school.

"Brian?" she squeaked.

He looked up from buttoning his shirt, stepped closer. "Hands off, buddy, the lady is mine."

Her breath caught in her chest, and she

recognized at that moment he realized what he had said, because he snatched his gaze from her and pretended to pay attention to his buttons again.

She worked up enough courage and grabbed her own semidry clothing, shrugged into it piece by piece, careful to keep a few feet between herself and the orangutan. "What does he want?"

"Who knows." Brian reached his hand toward the animal. "He's just probably curious."

The next second, without warning, the orangutan rushed up the nearest tree, startling her into a small scream. He disappeared from sight as quick as he had appeared.

"What was that about?" she asked, and heard gunfire in the distance just as the last word was out.

"We have to go." Brian jumped to the canoe.

She made quick work of dressing and went to help him. It wasn't easy. She kept slipping in the mud. Dammit. She scraped the back of her hand, but ignored the burn.

The guns sounded closer and closer.

Then the canoe was free, and they carried it toward the river, making slow progress between the trees.

Brian dropped the front finally. "We'd be sitting ducks on the water," he said, his face mirroring his frustration.

"Can we hide until they pass?" She set down the back end and jumped when a succession of shots banged through the air somewhere nearby.

Whoever was shooting, she didn't think they were shooting at Brian and her. They were too far still. But they weren't poachers, either. She had shot a semiautomatic rifle when she'd gone after Brian to Hamid's camp, and that's what the shots sounded like now, coming fast together.

He looked at her, back at the canoe, hesitated for a moment, then grabbed her hand and lurched forward.

"Run!"

Chapter Ten

They scampered through the forest, careful to make as little noise as possible, ducking under vines, zigzagging around obstacles. Audrey was gasping the humid air when they stopped a few minutes later. But at least they had managed to put some distance between them and the gunfire that seemed to come from every direction.

"Sounds like a major offensive." Brian scoured the woods.

A loud boom of some serious weapon punctuated his last word, coming from the east.

She jumped closer to him. "What was that?"

The tight set of his shoulders relaxed,

and he flashed an unexpected grin at her. "The army."

"How do you know?" She held her soaring hope in check. Could it be so simple? Could rescue be just around the corner?

"That was a rocket launcher, not your standard guerilla ammo. It's too cumbersome to carry around in the jungle and not much use with the limited visibility the trees impose. Let's go."

"Do you think they came for the hostages?" She hurried to keep up with him as he moved forward, even passed him after a while, eager to spot their saviors. "We've done it, haven't we? They will protect us and send word of the KL attack."

"With some luck. We have to be very careful, though." And as if to punctuate his words, he grabbed her and pulled her back, shoved her behind him.

She gasped at his uncharacteristic roughness. "You don't have to—" Then she saw something move on the branch that a second ago had been inches from her face.

A snake.

"Don't move." Brian stood perfectly still, as the snake stared at them and lifted its head, ready to strike.

Her blood thundered in her ear. How on earth had she missed that? It was at least five feet, although hard to tell exactly since its length was draped, and in some sections coiled, around the gnarly branch.

"Is it poisonous?" She barely breathed the words.

"Move back slowly."

She couldn't. She was as paralyzed as if she'd been bitten. All she could think of was Joey, her aunt's German shepherd that had gotten into a fight with a rattler during one of the summers she had spent with her aunt in Texas, and the painful death the poor dog had died, despite all intervention.

"Don't look at the snake. Look at your feet." Brian's voice was full of patience.

It reached her on some level. She had to move. He was in front of her and couldn't pull back until she did. He had put himself into harm's way for her once again. She took a deep, shuddering breath and pushed one foot back, then the other.

"You're doing fine, keep going."

The sound of gunfire filled the air again. They were so close. The army was here. They were as good as saved, and could tell them where the hostages were. Nicky could be back in Kuala Lumpur by tonight, and she with her, and Brian. She pushed away the panic that gripped her limbs and did as Brian had asked.

"I'm petrified of snakes," she said after they had gotten far enough to move normally and resumed their trek. She was watching every branch now, every spot she set her feet, instead of blindly following Brian, getting lost in her thoughts as she had earlier.

"They didn't seem to bother you before." He glanced back.

"Before?"

"When we passed them." He turned his attention to the woods again, led the way around a patch of giant root buttresses.

The muscles in her legs went weak. She pulled her neck in, feeling all of a sudden that the trees above them were full of nasty things just waiting to drop on her shoulders. She tugged the new leaf-hat he'd made her earlier firmly into place. Snakes. She hadn't seen them before. She'd been too busy thinking about Nicky, and surviving to the next day. She had been focused on Brian.

"It might not have been poisonous," he said over his shoulder. "I don't remember seeing that kind before. There must be a hundred species of snakes on Borneo, I doubt anyone but the local tribes know all of them."

Great. That information made her feel so much better. There were things she simply didn't need to know. She shivered in the heat, her skin covered in goose bumps from thinking about a hundred different snakes.

The gunfight ebbed, then started up again. The closer they got, the slower they went.

"You better stay here," Brian said after a couple of hundred feet. "This is going to be tricky."

"No," she said without thinking, as the panic she had just conquered, slammed into her midsection again. "I don't want to stay alone."

He looked at her for a long moment then drew her in for a tight hug. "I hate the thought of leaving you behind, but they might shoot at me. Hell, they probably will. Things could get dangerous."

"What isn't?"

She lifted her face to him, and realized that more than she was scared of snakes and other jungle perils, more than she was scared of being left alone, she was scared for him. What if something happened to him and she wasn't there to help? "We're a team. I'm coming."

He watched her for a long moment, brushed his lips against her forehead suddenly, then let her go. "Okay. But only because I don't think it's safe to leave you tied to a tree. Stay behind me at all times."

She smiled at him and filled her lungs.

They crept from cover to cover, bush to bush. Then the vegetation thickened as they came to the edge of a swollen creek. The army was on the other side. She couldn't see them, but the gunfire was close enough for her to want to stay flattened to the ground.

Then after a while, the guns fell silent.

"I'm going to try to make contact," he said, and led her to a large rock boulder. "You wait for me. I'm not going far."

She began to protest, but he silenced her with a look. "This part is not negotiable."

"Don't take any chances."

He looked at her with humor in his startling blue eyes. "I think it's a little too late for that."

He dropped to his stomach and crawled to the trees on the side of the creek. From her vantage point she could see both him and the other side. Then the leaves began to move over there. The army was coming. She could see the first soldier hack through the jumble of vines.

More came, scanning the jungle, their guns in front of them, ready.

Brian stripped off his shirt, stuck it out on a stick, a makeshift "white flag" that was dirty brown. "Americans," he yelled the single word at the same time, but it was no use.

They started shooting as soon as the first syllable was out. And they did a thorough job of it. She didn't have to be told to run. Brian pointed south, scrambling toward her, and she sprinted, pushed by a strong sense of self-preservation.

"Not too trigger-happy, are they?" she said when they were far enough so they could stop to catch their breath.

"They're in the middle of a fight. They're gonna shoot at everything that moves. Can't say I blame them. Still, I had to give it a try."

She was drowning in disappointment. It didn't work. Their best hope for survival was a bust.

"What are we going to do?" Without the canoe their mission was doomed, and they definitely couldn't go back that way to retrieve it. "Maybe if I went to them. They wouldn't shoot at a woman, would they?"

"Don't even think about it. We'll wait until nightfall, then I'll sneak into their camp and disarm a guard. I'll explain what's going on, so he can call off the rest. Then they can radio in what we have on KL and call in help to pick up your sister and the others."

It sounded feasible, not that she felt comfortable with it, but it had been a while since she had felt comfortable with anything. Brian had proven to her over and over again that he was capable, that he knew what he was doing. She had to trust him. And she did. "Sounds like a plan. What do we do in the meanwhile?"

"Find food and shelter. But if they move on, we're going to have to follow them." He took off his belt and jumped to the ground, ripped off his shirtsleeve, rolled it up.

"What are you doing?" Then she saw the dark patch on his pants. "You're shot!"

She dropped to her knees next to him, pressed the rolled-up cloth to the wound while he tied the belt in place to keep the pressure on.

"It's your good leg." Her gaze flew to his. God, it was so unfair.

"Just a flesh wound. Nothing serious." He smiled at her. "If all goes well, tomorrow morning they'll be airlifting us out."

She had to believe that. Because no way could Brian make it out of the jungle like this. And neither would she without him.

"Come on." He grabbed her hand and stood with her. "We have a lunch date with some grubs."

She wiped his blood on her pants and went with him, food being the last thing on her mind for once. He was injured. Reality was still sinking in. His injury changed everything. They no longer had the option of walking away from the army and trying to make it out of the jungle on their own. He needed help, and he needed it fast.

He grabbed a fallen branch to help him support his weight as he walked, and she watched his more pronounced limp. "Do you think this is going to work?"

"We'll make it work."

"What if the army…" She couldn't bring herself to finish the sentence, but her doubts echoed in her head. What if they couldn't make contact? What if the army attacked them thinking they were the enemy?

"If they get me before I can talk to them, I want you to find the river and follow it out of the jungle. Once you get down far enough there'll be some villages. Somebody will have a cell phone or a radio." His voice was thick. He didn't turn around to look at her.

"It's not going to happen," she rushed to say, wishing she had kept her fears to herself.

"I hope not, but it could. If there's one group trained as well in jungle warfare as mine, it's the Royal Malaysian Army. It's not gonna be easy to sneak up on them."

"But if I went to them? I'm a woman. I look foreign." She wished he would consider that as an option.

"They'd be shooting at you long before they saw you. They're at high alert, in the middle of an offensive. I shouldn't have tried to approach them at the creek. It was a mistake. If you end up on your own and meet up with soldiers, don't move toward them unless you have a large enough open area where you can come at them from far away. Walk with your hands high in the air, or down on your knees with your hands linked behind your head. Whatever you do, don't surprise them."

He stopped by a fallen log and lifted it, holding it with both hands.

She was trying to form an argument, but

the foot-long centipede he'd uncovered stopped her thoughts. A long moment passed before she realized he was probably waiting for her to pick it up. "I'll chew off my own arm before I'm eating that."

But his attention wasn't on what was under the log.

He shook his head, nodded toward the woods, then slowly lowered the chunk of deadwood. What? She listened and heard the soft noise. A small deer, no bigger than a hare, stumbled from the bushes. It stared at them, drummed on the ground with its feet that were literally the length and thickness of a pencil, then darted to the right.

Brian lunged and threw himself at the animal, but he'd been too far, his legs not having enough power for the move. He missed by a foot, and the deer took off into the woods with dazzling speed.

"Damn." He groaned as he got up.

"Are you hurt?" She was at his side the next second, supporting him. Stupid question. Of course he was hurt. Fresh blood seeped through his pants. "Don't do that again."

He pulled away, as if he was embarrassed, and shrugged. "We need to eat."

"Was it a fawn? It was tiny. I can't believe how fast it ran." Although its head, legs and coloring were that of a deer, its body was rounder, strangely formed.

He found his stick and leaned on it. "A mouse deer," he said. "That's as big as they get. It would have made a fine dinner."

She'd only had venison once before and didn't particularly take to it, but the idea of real food, meat, made saliva gather in her mouth. Her stomach growled. She kicked up some leaf mold and found a half-dozen beetle-like bugs, with alternating brilliant red and blue stripes. "How about these?"

"Probably not a good bet. Bright color is usually a warning sign that they're poisonous."

She watched the bugs burrow into the dirt as she stood. She wasn't all that disappointed. "Maybe we'll come across some fruit."

But they didn't. It took another half an hour before they found a handful of grubs that were good to eat. And since the skies opened again by then, they washed down their lunch with some rainwater. When they were done, Brian helped her up a tree and wove some leaves together over them—not a terribly effective shelter, but the best they could do under the circumstances.

He sat in the V where the branch met the trunk, with his arms around her. Her back soaked up his heat, and she let her head fall onto his shoulder. His leg was elevated on a cross branch.

"How is it?"

"I'm glad this happened now and not before. We're almost out of here."

He took off the belt and checked his injury. It was no longer bleeding. His blood had clotted, the makeshift bandage stuck in the wound. He tore off his other sleeve and ripped it into a long strip, tied it around what was already there. "This should keep the dirt out."

She put her hands over his, wanting to hold on to him.

"Tonight I'll make contact. We'll be out

of here in the morning," he said, as if sensing the despair that fought to take her over.

He was injured, dangerously so—even a minor wound could get infected enough to become a life threatening problem in the jungle. And yet he thought not of himself, but how to set her at ease. His strength had a way of strengthening her, as if they shared some invisible link.

"So tell me about this kid of yours," he said in a transparent attempt to take her mind off their problems.

And she did, to distract him from his. "Her name is Mei. Her mother is Chinese-Malaysian and she's too young to keep her. She's so beautiful, Brian."

Tears gathered in her eyes as she thought of the small picture the agency had sent her, the one Omar's men had taken along with everything else that had been in her pockets.

"How old is she?"

"Three months." She smiled through her tears. She had not specified age or sex when contacting the adoption agency, but was overjoyed as soon as they told her they'd found her a baby girl.

"You'll be a good mother." He pressed his lips against her neck, and their warmth seemed to spread through her whole body. "You don't scare easily."

She smiled and touched her cheek against his, rough with the beginnings of another beard. They hadn't had a fire the night before to shave by, and during the day he never wasted time with it. She didn't mind.

"Did you scare your adoptive parents?"

He groaned. "Don't remind me. God, the torture I put them through."

She tried to picture him as a mischievous, carefree little boy and the picture that blossomed in her mind softened her heart.

"I was trouble with a capital T," he said.

"Probably not more than any other young boy."

"I was definitely a restless spirit."

She could hear the smile in his voice. "But they loved you anyway."

"Yeah, they did. I owe them a lot."

His words were full of so much love and tenderness toward those people, it made her heart skip a beat, wanting to be so good a mother that Mei would feel that way about her someday. She was beginning to see Brian in a different light from her first wild-man-of-the-jungle impression. There were layers and layers to the man, a complexity that went beyond his identity as a prisoner or soldier.

The sudden upswell of emotion that constricted her throat left her bewildered. "Why don't you sleep," she said. "I'll keep watch. You need to store your energy for tonight."

He kissed her temple without saying anything, but after a while, she could feel his even breathing. She felt absurdly safe in the cocoon of his arms. It was ridiculous. They were in the wilds of the jungle, in the middle of an armed confrontation, both sides of which would just as soon shoot them as look at them.

She stared into the rain, listened for the sound of gunfire, but couldn't hear any.

It made her nervous. What if the army was moving on? Should she wake Brian? Not yet. He needed rest. She would wait a few minutes. They might start fighting again and she would know then what their location was. Even if they moved, that many people would leave a wide enough trail to follow. She would let Brian be. Give him a chance to regain his strength.

She relaxed against him, and he mumbled something in his sleep. She squeezed her eyes shut. *Dear God. If only one of us can make it out of here alive, let it be him.*

He would have made it if it hadn't been for her and the madcap rescue of her sister. After what he had suffered in this jungle, she couldn't stand the thought of him dying here. She couldn't stand the thought of anything happening to him, period.

BRIAN INCHED FORWARD in the darkness. It had taken them an hour to find the soldiers, creeping toward where he'd last heard gunfire. He glanced back at the bushes that hid Audrey. Her instructions were to not to move a muscle until he came for her. She hadn't protested this time, a good thing since he didn't have the energy to fight her.

He stole forward, cursing the pain in his

legs. But he didn't mind that as much as he minded the fact that his injuries slowed him down. He had missed that deer earlier. What if it had been a bullet he'd been ducking from? He crawled another few feet. Where the hell were the guards? He was nearly in the camp.

He could see men sleeping on the ground in a haphazard pattern, but there was no fire and nobody watching. A trap? They couldn't have possibly known that he was coming. Were they baiting the guerillas? There was barely enough light to see the lumps of soldiers, no way to tell if they were grabbing their guns, watching from under hooded eyelids as he did. Then he was close enough to one of them to see the unnatural pose he was lying in.

Dead.

A cold feeling spread through Brian's stomach. He crawled over, alert to any noise or movement, and reached out, even though he could see now that the man's eyes stared blindly into the night. No pulse. His fingers came away sticky with blood. Damn. He'd been killed a while ago. And so had the rest of them. They wouldn't have simply gone to sleep with a bloody corpse in their midst, inviting predators. The lack of guards made sense now. There was no one alive for guard duty.

The guerillas had won the skirmish.

Brian swore under his breath. How many other army units were in the jungle? He didn't think the twenty or so men scattered around him was all. From the ruckus that had gone on all day long, he figured a larger force.

Where were the rest camping? He came to his knees, ready to go back to Audrey and break the bad news, hating to have to dash her hopes. But there was no sense in trying to do more right now, too dark to see. When the sun came up they could search the bodies for anything useful, then go and find the rest of the army. Then when night fell again, he would try the same approach.

A branch snapped in the woods to his right.

He threw himself to the ground, next to the dead body, and went still.

Where the hell was the man's gun? He

scanned the ground as a small group of guerillas walked out of the forest. Damn. Too late now. The rifle was probably under the soldier, and he couldn't move him without drawing attention.

His first thought was Audrey, hoping that she would stay down and stay quiet. He'd left her far enough behind. Unless the men began to really spread out, she should be fine.

But the guerillas didn't show any inclination to separate from each other. They walked through the carnage, lifting rifles, clipping hand grenades off the belts of the fallen. Why hadn't they made camp for the night? He watched, his eyes only slits. Maybe they had a camp somewhere nearby and were heading back to it. Darkness had just fallen.

A few tense minutes passed, then it seemed they were finally moving off.

In Audrey's direction.

His pulse quickened. A hundred feet and they would be right on top of her.

Brian grabbed a hand grenade from the body next to him, but he couldn't throw it into the group. They were too close to Audrey now, he couldn't risk hitting her with shrapnel. He judged the distance, aimed to throw it short. He still might wound a couple and it would certainly get their attention.

He pulled the ring and tossed the grenade, then took off running in the opposite direction, just as the explosion shook the night.

They came after him with a vengeance. He dashed through the forest, ignoring the pain that throbbed through his legs and made him trip a few times.

Go. Go. Go.

He couldn't outrun them, but he hoped he could lead them away from Audrey enough so they wouldn't bother going back that way.

She would make it out. He had to believe that beyond anything else, because that was the only thing that kept him going.

He ducked behind a tree and leaned against it to catch his breath, and could hear them gaining on him. He darted forward. Just a little more. Just a little more.

Then they must have spotted him, because bullets began to fly.

Damn, he hated to leave her alone. He scanned the ground for somewhere to hide. If he weren't injured he could have gotten far enough ahead to lose them. He ducked behind a tree again and drew his knife. He wasn't about to let them just pick him off as if they were on a deer hunt. He owed it to himself to go out fighting.

When his ears told him they were right on him, he jumped out and threw himself on the closest man, buried the blade in his chest, then before the rest could react he was on his feet, ready to face the next.

He lunged for the guy, but a loud crack split his skull. It seemed literally. He felt like he was falling, but not just the short distance to the ground. His last thought was Audrey, that if she followed his advice and fled for the river, there was still hope for her.

People were talking around him, but it was all a ringing noise in his ears. When darkness came, more complete than even the jungle could produce, he didn't fight it. He had done what he could.

Chapter Eleven

Something had gone wrong. There wasn't supposed to be a fight.

Audrey crept forward from her hiding place, listening for anything suspicious, hoping she would hear Brian calling to her. She had waited all night in the bushes for him to return for her. Instead, there'd been an explosion, then gunfire that moved off into the distance.

The only logical explanation she could come up with was that the soldiers had discovered Brian before he managed to make contact and they had pursued him. Not a large group, judging from the sound of their guns. She hadn't dared move all night, fearing they'd left some men behind, not wanting to break the promise she'd given Brian about staying put and staying safe. But the sun was coming up now, and she needed to find out what had happened.

She moved in a crouch, careful where she put her feet, watching for small branches on the ground that would snap under her weight. If she did make noise, she stopped and waited several seconds like she had learned from Brian.

The overnight downpour had stopped at dawn, but now and then a fat splatter of water still landed on her hat or shoulders, making its way down from the leaves above. It startled her each time, but she kept quiet and focused on the woods ahead of her.

She heard no voices, no movement, no man-made noise of any kind. It filled her with unease. She was sure she was close enough and the soldiers would be awake by now. Surely there were at least a few left behind to guard their camp.

And then she could see them on the ground through the leaves, and they were obviously dead. All of them.

Had Brian done this? Confusion swept

through her. No, he couldn't have. He didn't have a gun. But then what had happened?

She hesitated, unsure of what to do. The sun was up. Brian had said if he hadn't returned by daylight she was to make her way to the river on her own. And yet she couldn't make herself walk away.

Watching for the slightest sign of danger, she came out into the open. Whatever she decided to do, her chances of survival would be better if she had a weapon. Strangely, the first couple of men she looked over, didn't have their rifles anywhere near.

Then she did see a gun, a pistol next to a body a little farther off. She walked among the dead and picked it up, tucked it into her belt. A few broken branches caught her eye. Somebody, a bunch of people, had rushed through this way. Had they been pursuing Brian?

Did she dare attempt to follow the track? Could she follow it? She knew nothing about tracking beyond the obvious. Right now she had a fair idea in which direction the river was and it wasn't far away. But if she ran off blindly, got turned around, lost her way…

Brian was in trouble. If the tables were turned he'd be on his way by now to save her, instead of sitting around weighing his options.

There was an extra clip of bullets on the man's belt and she reached for it, even though she had no idea how to put them in the gun. But by God, she would figure it out.

A slight sound reached her ear and she froze, almost dismissed it when it came again. Something was moving in the bushes on the other side of the field of bodies—something big.

She flattened herself to the ground behind a trio of basketball-size rocks, hoping those and some overhanging vines camouflaged her enough. She saw a flash of yellow.

The tiger came out into the open and looked among the bodies, meandering, sniffing. He didn't seem to be in any hurry. Audrey held her breath as the animal moved in her direction.

Stay still. Stay still. She repeated the

words in her head, although they were unnecessary, her limbs truly and completely frozen with fear.

The tiger stopped a good thirty feet from her and let out a rumbling, coughing sound that scared her witless and squeezed her insides until she thought she would wet her pants. Then the animal locked his tremendous jaw over the shoulder of the man in front of him and dragged the body into the forest.

She began to shake, her stomach revolting at the sight of the soldier's disappearing feet. She could hear the noise of the body being dragged on the ground for a while. Some time passed before she could get up, move. She took a few steps into the opposite direction, then leaned against a tree and threw up water, the only thing that had been in her stomach.

Survival instinct gave her strength and pushed her forward. She clawed her way through some vines, then saw another body a short way ahead. This one was dressed differently than the soldiers. She walked closer and paled when she recognized him.

He was one of the guerillas who had captured her in the village at the beginning of her journey.

And the dead soldiers made sense all of a sudden. The guerillas had won the fight with the army. They were the ones who gave chase to Brian.

She tipped the body over with the toe of her boot, saw the familiar knife sticking out of the man's chest. Brian had gotten one of them. She pulled the knife, looked up to where she could barely make out a track in front of her and started forward again.

She'd gone no more than a hundred feet when she spotted a pair of boots sticking out of the bushes, similar enough to Brian's to make her heart lurch. She moved closer to investigate, her hands shaking from relief when she pulled the branches aside and looked into the face of a stranger. He was a soldier, apart from the others. Had he run when it became obvious that they were losing the fight? Her gaze caught on the top of a backpack that peeked from under the body.

He was covered in blood, his whole chin

missing, taken off by a bullet probably. She heaved again, but there was nothing in her stomach to bring up. She didn't want to touch him.

Brian would.

He would leave no resource behind that might save their lives. Who knew what was in the bag—food, a map, matches. She took a deep breath and rolled the body, tried to pull off the backpack, but the man's arms had stiffened into an angle that made it impossible for her to work the straps. She pulled her knife and cut them.

She dragged the backpack away from the body before she opened it, pushed aside the clothes on top and gasped at the sight of a compact radio unit. There was something else too, a smaller electronic device that looked like one of those hand-held organizers. She pushed the red button and some kind of a picture came up with numbers. Not just any numbers, she realized after a moment—coordinates. She had a GPS unit, Global Positioning System, that showed exactly where she was.

She knew her location and had the

means to call for help. She sank to the ground as tears of relief filled her eyes. But the feeling of optimism didn't last long. Nothing but static came through the radio when she turned it on, no matter which way she twisted the dial.

Brian would know what to do with it. He could be even now lying somewhere in the woods, wounded. She turned off both units, threw them into the backpack and got up, started out again.

She didn't have to go far before she came across the spot where the men had camped for the night. She had not found Brian's body so far. But she knew his pursuers wouldn't have rested unless they had caught him. Which meant, he was most likely once again a prisoner. God knew what they were doing to him. She pushed on.

She didn't stop again until she had to relieve herself. She was weak with hunger, but at least no longer cold. Although her clothes were still damp, the temperature had risen enough to be comfortable. She opened the backpack and turned on the radio, turned the dial slowly, from one end of the spectrum to the other.

Then finally she found something, a man talking rapidly in another language.

"Hello." She grabbed the speaker. "I need help," she said, and realized there was probably a button somewhere she needed to push to transmit. She found a rubbery spot on the side of the receiver and pushed that in. "I need help," she repeated, her heart in her throat.

Silence.

Oh, she probably had to let go of the button. She did so, and the response came after a few seconds.

"Identify yourself. Out."

"I'm an American. I'm lost in the jungle. My partner was taken by guerillas."

A longer period of silence this time.

"How did you get this radio? Out."

"I found a group of dead soldiers a while back. They're a few miles from the river." She fished the GPS out, turned it on and read the displayed numbers to the man.

"Stay where you are. I'm sending a man to get you. Out."

She thought of Brian, that he might be injured, what Omar's men might be doing to him. "I'm going to follow the guerillas. I'll let you know where I am again in an hour."

To her surprise, the man didn't protest or forbid her. "Let us know as soon as you spot them. Don't try to approach them. We'll be there as fast as we can. Out."

She thanked him and turned off the radio and the GPS, wanting to save the batteries and not wanting the static from the radio to alert anyone to her approach.

Despite the shade the trees provided, the rising heat got to her more and more as the day wore on. Walking in the jungle was drastically different without Brian. It was much scarier and savage, and she had no one to distract her from it.

The sound of a single shot made her duck into the bushes before her brain registered that it came from far enough away not to pose an immediate threat. At least it confirmed that she was still going in the right direction. The tracks she'd been following had crossed an old animal trail a while back and since that point she no longer had broken plants to guide her. She hoped the guerillas had followed the trail, instead of having simply crossed it and covering their tracks.

When she saw a body slumped against a tree up ahead, she kept walking toward it, thinking it was another casualty, then his hand twitched, and she realized the young guerilla was sleeping, probably on guard duty.

She stepped off the trail, behind a tree, and waited. Nothing. She peeked out. It didn't look like he'd moved. She crept forward in the woods, keeping the trail in sight, glancing back frequently at the man.

She didn't have to go far before she heard noises up ahead. She radioed in her GPS location, not daring to raise her voice above a whisper, then shut off the radio. Bugs be damned, she got into the thickest of the brush for optimum coverage, moving forward one slow step at a time. Her progress was excruciating, not only because the dense vegetation held her back, but because she waited after each step to make sure she wasn't discovered.

The closer she got to them the slower she went, until inch by inch she finally reached the edge of a clearing and, laying under a shiny-leaved bush, she was able to see the men. There were a lot of them. She counted about a hundred. Were the various groups uniting?

Then someone she recognized stepped into the clearing, and her heart tripped. Omar.

She watched as he talked to a couple of the men, then walked around. She inched forward another foot to see where he was going. And then she saw Brian.

Oh, God. The emotions that washed through her at the sight were strong enough to take her breath away. What had they done to him? He was hanging by his tied hands from a tree, his feet barely touching the ground. His pants on one leg were completely soaked in blood, and his face was bloody, too, on the right side. She watched helplessly, with fury screaming inside, as Omar walked over to him and smashed the butt of his rifle against Brian's ribs.

He didn't cry out. Instead, he lifted his head an inch or two and looked right at her.

Could he see her? She scooted back. If Brian could spot her, then so could the others. Not that anyone was looking hard. The men were eating and talking, lounging around camp as if they didn't have a care in the world. No doubt they thought there was safety in their number.

Omar hit Brian over and over, then stopped to talk to him. She wished she could hear what he said as he played with the rifle. There was such a look of madness in his face.

He was going to kill Brian, she realized, and grabbed her pistol, closing one eye and concentrating on her aim. She pulled back what she thought was the safety and steadied her hand. There was a better-than-good chance that she was going to miss, but even if all she managed to do was cause a distraction, it could give Brian enough time to break free.

But just as she put her finger on the trigger, a hand came over her mouth, another pulled the pistol from her, the weight of a man pressing her to the ground.

Her first instinct was to struggle, but her brain kicked in on time and she held still. If a guerilla discovered her, he wouldn't have held her mouth. He wouldn't have cared if she made noise.

The army?

She glanced back at the clearing to see if they'd noticed anything and her blood froze. Omar had turned the rifle around and was resting the barrel against Brian's temple. He was still talking to him.

The man half on top of her tugged her back, and she moved with him. He let go of her mouth, and she could turn at last to look at him. A soldier. It *was* the army. They were finally here.

"Are you the American?" he asked when they were at a safe distance.

"You have to save that man," she said, and saw the rest of the soldiers.

The man gave them a signal and they moved ahead without a sound.

"You stay here. I've got many questions

for you when I get back," he said, and went after them.

Brian was tied up, immobile and defenseless in the middle of a shootout. And she was going to sit here and wait? *Unlikely.*

Audrey rushed back toward the camp, circling it, hoping to reach the other side and Brian in time. She didn't have to be careful about noise now, the sound of gunfire was deafening in the air. Didn't have to worry about wild animals, either. The ruckus was sure to scare them far away from the place. She ran as fast as she could.

Omar came out of the bushes at a dead run, looking backward, barreling right into her, sending them both sprawling to the ground. She grunted, the air knocked out of her lungs by the impact, struggled to get up and get away from him. But he made it to his feet first and had his knife pulled from his belt the next second.

"Move." He dragged her up with the blade to her throat and yanked her forward, deeper into the jungle.

"No. Wait." She fought him, her hands on the arm that held the knife, but he was the stronger one between the two of them. "You can go faster without me. You don't need me."

But then as he sunk to his knee, she realized he was injured. Blood gushed from his side above the right hip. And still, he kept a good strong grip on her.

He probably knew he wasn't going to get far and wanted to use her as a shield when the army caught up with him. It wasn't the army that reached them first.

"Let her go." Brian stepped out from behind a tree. He had to be weak with blood loss, too, but he showed no sign of it.

His eyes were as cold as the blade Omar held against her throat, and the predatory flow with which he moved, closer and closer, more menacing than the tiger had been. She felt Omar shift behind her.

"Come one step closer and she's dead," he said.

"She gets as much as nicked and I'll tear you apart from limb to limb." Brian's gaze was fixed on the man, his voice so deadly, it made her shiver despite the heat.

She'd seen him in rough-soldier mode

before, but she'd never seen him like this. He was tightly controlled, yet there was a glint of madness in his gaze, a ferocious darkness.

The blade pressed against her skin. She didn't dare move when Omar tightened his hold on her. He was breathing hard and sweating, not nearly as confident now that Brian wasn't tied up and helpless before him.

Brian advanced on them, the sight as paralyzing as that of the tiger had been. And Omar must have felt the same, because he didn't move, didn't cut her as he had threatened, even as he repeated, "Stop. Don't come any closer." His words had little strength now, they were underlined with fear.

Then the next thing she knew, Brian lunged at them, flying through the air as he attacked. She was knocked aside, and rolled away. By the time she looked back, the two men were locked in a deadly battle. Omar still had the knife but Brian was gripping his wrist, as they wrestled for control.

Brian came to be on bottom somehow, holding Omar off, trying to shove away the sharp blade aimed at his throat. And then he did, twisting the knife and letting his arms go lax. Omar's weight, suddenly released, pushed the blade through his own heart.

He died with a groan of disbelief torn from his throat, his eyes rounded as if in surprise.

Brian shoved the man off without another look at him and rushed to her. "Are you hurt?"

He looked her over, then when she shook her head, unable to speak, he crushed her to him.

"How is your leg?" she asked finally when the wave of emotions in her began to settle.

"Barely bleeding."

She examined the wound at his temple that didn't seem as bad up close as she had thought when she'd first seen it, a lot less damage than the blood suggested.

"A bullet got too close." He lifted his fingers to the spot she was looking at. "Head wounds bleed like a bastard."

"Hang on." She walked over to Omar, ripped the flask off his belt and went back to Brian to wash the side of his face.

She used the corner of her shirt, and when she was done with his skin, she rubbed the dried blood out of his hair. He could have used a stitch or two, but probably he'd be all right without it.

Guns were still going off here and there, but the battle seemed to be nearing the end.

He ran a light finger over his temple. "When I saw you under that bush— Didn't I tell you to head for the river?"

"If I didn't follow you, I couldn't have given the army your coordinates. I found a radio." She smiled at the stunned look he gave her.

"You brought the army?"

Her smile widened into a grin.

"I should go help them," he said after a moment, but didn't move.

She burrowed against him, soaked up his strength, and gave thanks for the miracle that they were both alive. "Stay."

And he did.

He gave a strangled laugh and held her closer. "I've changed more than I realized," he said when she lifted her head and threw him a questioning look. "A couple of years ago, nothing and no one could have kept me from rushing back into the fray. Now, all I want to do is sit here and never let you go."

She told herself not to read too much into that even as her heart leaped. They'd been through a lot together. She was the first woman he'd seen in four years, for heaven's sake. A certain amount of attachment was natural and would probably wear off fast once he returned to the real world. She couldn't fall for him. Not now.

She was going to become a mother in a few days, that's what she needed to focus on. She couldn't get entangled in a relationship that had started out of mutual need under extreme conditions. Not even if she could have sworn she was losing her heart to the man. She would get over it. They both would.

She pulled away just as the soldier she'd talked to earlier came walking from the direction of the fight, a couple of men behind him. He stopped by Omar's body, then looked at them. "So who the hell are you?"

"Audrey Benedict. My sister is Nicky Brown, one of the tourists kidnapped by the guerillas."

"Brian Smith," Brian said, and smiled when the man drew up an eyebrow. "I'm a personal protection specialist hired by Miss Benedict."

She tried not to act surprised at his new last name and the rest of his words, but wasn't sure she altogether managed.

"What do you know about the hostages?"

"They escaped the guerillas two days ago and headed for an Orang Ulu village. I can give you a fair approximate location."

The man nodded. "We'll pick them up." He turned to her. "You mentioned something about an attack in KL?"

She pulled the papers from her pocket and handed them to the man.

He looked through them. "Looks like you've been swimming."

"I have. But they were bad even before that. We were able to make out Kuala Lumpur and the date August tenth. This part here—" she stepped next to him and found the right sheet "—used to be a list of embassies."

"Call it in," he said to one of his men before turning back to her. "And you came by this how?"

"We were both captured by Omar. He wrote this to another guerilla leader, and we took it with us when we escaped," Brian said, pointing to one set of papers. "These I found at Hamid's camp where the hostages were." He indicated the rest.

"Right. We'll talk some more about this." He motioned to four of his soldiers and said something in Malay before switching back to English. "There's a new logging road about two miles east of here with enough space for the chopper to land. I'm giving you an escort there and sending you to KL for further questioning."

"And you'll send someone for the hostages?"

He nodded. "If you're cleared in KL, you'll be having dinner with your sister tonight."

She wasn't sure whether to laugh or cry. Nicky would be safe soon, the whole nightmare over. They'd be together again. But she was pretty sure that as soon as they got to Kuala Lumpur, Brian would be gone.

And as much as she knew that was for the best, she wasn't ready for it yet, reluctant to see him go.

There were still things unsaid between them. She could not possibly put her gratitude into words, and there were other feelings that were perhaps best left unsaid. She looked at him, hoping for a gesture, something to tell her what to do.

He smiled. "It's over."

She blinked hard, hating the words.

Chapter Twelve

He wasn't ready. He didn't know what to say.

Brian stood in front of the door of the hotel room, overwhelmed with sensory experiences. The hustle and bustle of the streets, the sheer size of the hospital where Audrey and he had been treated, even the clothes he wore, felt alien. Everything was too much, too loud, too new, too complicated.

He had spent the night watching television in his hospital room—the doctors had kept him overnight, but let Audrey go—and what he'd seen left him bewildered. He would have a lot to learn, a lot to catch up with. He didn't know anything, it seemed. No, not true. He knew one thing. He knew what he wanted.

Audrey.

He wanted her unequivocally, forever. He had enough time to think to know that he was in love with her.

And he loved her enough to want what was best for her. He was pretty sure it wasn't him.

He had no job, no money, nowhere to live. She deserved better. She deserved a carefree man who laughed a lot, not one who had years worth of dark memories to weigh him down. She deserved to sleep next to someone who wouldn't wake her up with his nightmares in the middle of the night.

And yet he was here. Not only to thank her for paying for his bill at the hospital and leaving him cash at the front desk. He wanted to see her one last time. He needed to see that she was okay. Then he would walk away.

He knocked even though he had a keycard. Audrey had left it in the envelope with the money.

She opened the door and stared at him for a moment. Blinked. "Brian…"

God, she looked beautiful. She had her

long hair down, the light gleaming off the golden strands that framed her face. She wore a pink figure-hugging sheath dress that made his mouth go dry. She was a different person. The grungy teammate who had fought her way through the jungle with him and ate grubs from the palm of his hand was gone. In her place, he found a dazzling woman, every inch a lady. Someone who took his breath away, but a woman he didn't recognize.

Her expression looked as stunned as he felt.

He glanced down at the pants and shirt he wore, and conscious of his yuppie haircut, ran his fingers through his hair. He hadn't meant to spend more of her money than it took to get to the hotel, but he had trouble with the doorman letting him in, taking him for a panhandler.

"You're so different..." The words rushed from her, before she caught herself.

And at last he looked past her clothes and found her eyes. Even they weren't the same. She had makeup on.

Something moved behind her and he had

her pushed aside, his body positioned to protect her, acting on instinct before he knew what he was doing.

The two men who came out of the kitchen area of the suite looked at him with suspicion.

"Audrey?" The taller of the two came forward.

"It's okay, Josh. This is Brian Smith, the man I told you about."

So this was the ex-husband. Brian extended his hand, not liking the way Josh seemed to measure him up. The man's handshake was firm, perhaps firmer than necessary, maybe a message he wanted to send. Brian resisted the urge to squeeze back hard, and pulled away before crossing the border of polite.

"My brother-in-law, Trevor," Audrey introduced the other guy, moving by him, making his head swirl with the flowery scent of her soap.

"I wanted to thank you for what you've done. I talked to Nicky this morning. They ended up taking the hostages to Miri yesterday to get checked out. It was the nearest hospital. But they'll be all here by to-night. She asked me to convey her grati-tude if I see you before she does."

Good to know some of the hostages, at least, felt that way. He'd caught coverage of that, too, the guy who had wanted to fight him for the boat, giving an interview about the reckless and irresponsible na-ture of the rescue, and the disrespect and lack of cooperation of the man who had come for them—a "hot-headed maverick," he'd said, "who took unnecessary chances with the lives of the hostages."

"You do this kind of thing often?" Josh was still checking him out.

"As often as necessary. I work in per-sonal security," he said, sticking to the story he'd invented the day before.

"Audrey is lucky to have found you," Trevor interjected.

He glanced at her from the corner of his eye. She looked flustered. "Is everything all right?"

"Sure," she said, but didn't look at him.

"She'll be fine now that we're here," Josh said, and stepped between them.

"I suppose you came for your fee." The brother-in-law offered him a beer out of the minibar.

Saliva gathered in his mouth. There had been times in the past couple of years when he would have given his soul for a cold beer. Now he waved it off. He wouldn't be here long enough to finish it.

"I'll be taking care of everything, of course." Trevor put the beer down and reached for his checkbook.

"It's all taken care of," he said. The suite felt small all of a sudden, and for a crazy moment he wished they were still back in the jungle.

"If you prefer cash we can get it by this afternoon and bring it over to your hotel," Josh said, putting his patrician nose where it didn't belong. "Where is it that you're staying?"

He didn't know yet. His first thought upon release had been to see Audrey. "No further payment is necessary."

He would get the money Colonel Wilson was sending to him at the embassy, crash in an airport hotel for the night, then leave on the first flight in the morning. He didn't belong here with these people. They belonged with each other.

"Mind if I use your phone?" he asked Audrey, then when she nodded, he called down and asked for reception to get him a cab to the embassy and call up when it was here. All he needed were a few minutes to say goodbye.

But Josh interrupted his call with, "The embassy is closed today. They all are. Some kind of credible terrorist threat or something."

Of course. August 10. He glanced at Audrey. How much had she told the men?

"We already tried to call earlier, to ask for their help. I missed my court date for the adoption hearing," she said.

Great. He had wanted to give the money back that she'd left for him at the hospital, but it seemed he would need to spend more of it. He hated it, and hated even more the uncertainty of the future. More of the same waited for him back home. He'd probably been declared dead long ago, his apartment rerented, the money in his bank account

God only knew where. What was the law for people who died without beneficiaries? The government probably had his savings by now.

"I will be—" He started to tell her that he would pay her back at the earliest opportunity, but Josh put his hand on the small of Audrey's back, and jealousy as hot and sharp as lightning nearly tore him in two. He wanted to kill the man, rip him apart. He had to leave. Now.

Audrey was safe with two men who obviously felt protective of her, one of whom was probably in love with her. They'd had their misunderstandings, but her ex obviously realized now what he had lost. And Josh was the kind of man she should have in her life. Brian clenched his jaw. What the hell did he have to offer?

He glanced at the clock on the wall without registering the time. "I'm late," he said. "I better get going." And with a nod to all three of them he walked out the door, not allowing as much as a goodbye look at her, not a handshake, nothing. If they touched, his heart might have shattered.

He put on numbness like he would have a uniform and, closing the door behind him, he walked away.

She deserves a normal life. He repeated it over and over to himself on the way down to the lobby, avoiding to look at his alien reflection in the mirrored walls of the elevator. He looked like a gentleman tourist instead of a soldier.

The unreasonable fury, the violent anger he felt toward Josh scared him. He wanted to kill the man for touching Audrey, for having a right to be in her hotel room.

He was no better than a wounded beast out for blood.

And that was exactly why he needed to protect Audrey from himself. Except—he thought—the emotions that nearly overwhelmed him weren't altogether unreasonable. He was a man, watching another guy take the woman he loved.

"She deserves a normal life," he murmured to himself. Josh was the right choice for her.

And then it hit him that he'd never given her that. Didn't she deserve a *choice?*

If he truly was a soldier, why wasn't he fighting for her instead of retreating?

HAMID WALKED TOWARD the elevator as the light came on. The door opened. There was one man in there, staring straight ahead. *The negotiator.*

Hamid turned to a guest room, presenting his back to the man, and knocked. He heard the elevator door close just as the door in front of him opened.

"Yes?" An older woman looked at him, her pencil-thin eyebrows drawn to mid-forehead as she took in his hotel uniform.

"You requested help with opening the extra bed, Madam?"

She looked baffled. "No. Certainly not."

"I apologize. I must have the wrong room number." He smiled cordially and walked away.

He didn't go back to the elevators to push the call button; he went to the stairs. That man could be staying at the hotel—an extreme case of bad luck—or he could be here for him.

Hamid ran over in his mind what he'd

seen in the lobby. No extra security, no sign that his plans had been discovered, that somebody was setting a trap. Still, he had to be careful. He took the stairs two at a time to the twenty-third floor where his men were setting up the second bomb in a linen supply closet.

AUDREY STOOD in the middle of the room, feeling as if a typhoon had swept through her soul. Josh and Trevor were talking, but she couldn't focus her mind on a single word. *Brian was gone.* Tears burned her eyes, threatening to spill. *Think about something else. Anything.*

"Are we still going downstairs to eat?" She said the first thing that came to her mind, although she couldn't have cared less about food at the moment, wasn't sure if she could swallow a bite.

Breathe in, breathe out.

"I was going to tell you just before that guy came in. Funny that he stopped by, isn't it?" Josh watched her. "With him having been already paid and all. I hope he didn't form some unnatural attachment to you." He shook his head. "Anyway, the restaurant, even the ballroom, are closed to the public today. There's some huge reception going on. The German ambassador finished off his term and he's going back home, and the other diplomats and whatnot are giving a big send-off party. But there are plenty of great places in the city." He smiled and took her hand.

She barely registered his words. "Would you guys mind if we ordered in? I don't really feel up to going out."

"Sure."

"Of course."

The tears were coming. She backed away. It wasn't as if she was embarrassed to cry in front of them, it was that she didn't want to have to explain why she was crying when everything was finally back to being good as far as they were concerned. Nicky would be here soon.

"You order, I'll grab some ice." She picked the ice bucket off the counter and turned as the first tear spilled.

"I can get it." Josh was right behind her.

"I don't mind," she said. "I need to

stretch my legs." And then she was out the door, relieved when he didn't follow.

She leaned against the wall and let out a big shivering breath. Brian was gone.

She had expected it, of course, but still it seemed too sudden. She hadn't anticipated how hard it would hit her. She had thought maybe— What? That he would ask for her phone number? That when their lives settled back at home, they could— She couldn't even finish the sentence. It seemed ridiculous now.

He left. Like that. What they had shared meant nothing to him. God, it meant the world to her. She had been what? Swift release after years of forced abstinence?

Tears washed down her face and she hiccupped. She wiped her eyes with the back of her hand. She'd always been a messy crier. The elevator dinged. Someone was coming to their floor. She headed for the staircase, not wanting to be seen like this.

She set the ice bucket down and leaned against the railing, took a couple of calming breaths that didn't help at all. The sound of footsteps came from above.

Someone was coming down the stairs. Wasn't there any place she could get some privacy?

She looked up and saw a waiter. What was he doing in the staircase? He greeted her politely and she nodded to him. Then her gaze fell to his right arm, left bare by the short-sleeved white uniform shirt. A giant crowned tiger lunged on his tattooed skin.

Hamid?

They were here. The ambassador's gala. It all made sense in a flash.

She gripped the railing and must have emitted some noise, because the man looked back at her. She made for the door, but he was already there, pulling a handgun from the back of his waistband.

A month ago, she would have screamed, and if her legs weren't shaking too hard for the job, she would have tried to run. But the jungle had changed her. She rushed the man instead, bent her waist and slammed into his midsection, pushing him against the door. He dropped the gun, probably more from surprise than the force of her attack, and they both dove for it, reaching it at the same time.

She did scream then, putting her full lung capacity to good use. "Help!"

But it was too late, he was gaining the upper hand fast, rolling her under him, bending her arm until the barrel was pointing at her head.

Blood stained the white shirt on his shoulder. There was murder in his eyes.

"Brian!" she screamed again, on instinct before she realized it was no use, he was already gone.

And then like an apparition, he was there, lifting Hamid off her and throwing him down the stairs. The man rolled but came up quick at the landing. He still had the gun and aimed it at Brian.

"If you shoot, it will echo enough in this staircase for everyone to hear. You'll never make it down without being caught," she said, desperate to distract him enough for Brian to make some kind of a move.

Hamid kept the gun on him. "The people of this country would rise up to support me if I were caught. They want what I want, to be rid of the foreign dogs and their support for the false king." He spat. "When

I win, there'll be celebrations on the streets."

She backed away, giving Brian room to maneuver. "If you do this, there'll be chaos and fear. Foreign investors will pull out, jobs will be lost, your people will suffer," she argued to keep his attention.

Hamid sneered at her. "Pain is necessary for growth."

"There are Malaysians in this hotel, guests and employees, as many as foreigners."

"They die as heroes." He braced the gun with both hands.

This was it. She snapped her head around, looked up as if she'd heard someone coming down the stairs above them. By the time she looked back, Brian was flying through the air, lunging at the man. Her ploy had worked. She'd distracted him long enough.

She rushed after Brian, but by the time she reached them they were tangled together, growling with effort to gain control of the weapon. Help. She needed to get help. She turned to rush back to the suite. Hamid heaved against Brian and smacked his bad knee to the railing. His hand slipped on the gun.

No time to go anywhere. He needed help now. When he turned, she threw herself on Hamid's head, thinking to cut off his air, or at the least, obstruct his vision. He bit her stomach. The sharp pain distracted her for a moment.

"Get away from here." Brian was pushing against her with his shoulder.

But she twisted finally and gained some leverage, smashed her elbow into Hamid's face with all her strength. She heard his nose break and thought she might be sick. She drew a deep breath, struck again. "That's for my sister."

And then she heard Brian laugh, and she turned to him just as he got up, holding the gun. Hamid wasn't moving.

"I love it when you talk tough," he said, and pulled her to him. "I can't believe you beat him unconscious."

She did? She glanced at Hamid, then back at Brian, horrified at first, then relieved. "I did. I'm not a violent person, but he just pushed me over the edge."

"You don't have to explain it to me, honey." He brushed his lips against hers. "Are you okay?" he asked even as he was stepping away from her to tie up Hamid with his belt and throw him over his shoulder.

"You came back."

"I love you. I'm going to want to talk to you about that when this is over." He started up the stairs, but when she followed, too stunned to respond, he shook his head. "I'm going to dump him out in the hallway so he doesn't block the stairs."

"All the ambassadors are downstairs," she blurted, as the thought cut through the rest of the confused jumble in her head.

"Where was he coming from?" Brian opened the door, took Hamid out, then came back in a split second.

"Upstairs."

"I want you to start walking down. Go as fast as you can. When you reach the lobby, pull the fire alarm." He handed her the pistol. "If you see anyone you recognize from our little vacation in the woods, shoot first, ask questions later."

Her brain was still on *"I love you."* Then he started up the stairs and it snapped her back to the here and now.

"Shouldn't we sound the alarm right away?"

He shook his head. "As soon as we do, people will flood the stairs. I need a couple of minutes to see if I can find the rest of the men, or at least one of them, and get a location on that bomb. If it's already set, there might not be enough time to get the hotel evacuated. Our best bet is to find the damn thing so I can disarm it."

"You can do that?"

"Trust me," he said.

And she did. "I should tell Trevor and Josh."

"There's no time for explanations, Audrey. Would you rather try to save two or everyone?"

She nodded and opened her mouth to tell him she loved him, too, but he was already gone. She flew down the stairs, taking them two and three at a time. They had a hotel full of people to save. And they were just the team to do it.

WHERE WAS HE? Audrey scanned the crowd behind the police line. She'd spotted Trevor and Josh on the other side of the square filled with hundreds of hotel guests, but she couldn't see Brian anywhere.

Josh was making his way over to her. Great.

"Thank God." He put his arms around her when he reached her.

She pulled away.

"Look," he said. "I didn't just come here as Trev's friend. I came because of you, too."

"Josh, I—"

"I missed you," he interrupted her. "I thought about this. You don't have to adopt. We can find an egg donor who'd be willing to be a surrogate mother. The baby would still be mine."

"It's not going to work."

"Why not? I'm willing to overlook—"

"I'm in love with another man."

The look on his face was priceless. Clearly, this was not something he had ever considered.

She left him and pushed through the sea of people to the front, from where she could see the hotel's main door. They'd been out here for an hour. The bomb-sniffing dogs were inside, going from floor to floor, the bomb squad robot waiting on the sidewalk for his turn once the bomb was found.

She had told everything she knew to the police at least four times, and they'd finally let her go. And now she had nothing else to do but obsess over the man she loved.

Then she saw him coming through the front doors, and yelled his name. He stopped, scanned the crowd, spotted her when she waved.

"Got a job?" She pointed to the security tag on his shirt when he came over.

He drew up an eyebrow. "I found it. This way I don't have to stop every five seconds, explaining to someone what I'm doing here."

All right, so he wasn't a strictly go-by-the-rules type of person. She kind of liked that about him.

He pulled her through the police line and nobody questioned them. She threw herself into his arms, not caring about the horde of reporters and TV cameras trained on the building and at them.

"Come here." He pulled her toward a side entrance, one that led to the restaurant. He flashed his badge to the officer at the door and they were let in without questions. He locked the door behind them.

"What happened?"

"We got the bombs. There were two of them—both disarmed now. They already took out Hamid and his men through the back. They're taking the bombs next and then as soon as the staircase is cleaned they're going to let people back in."

"Cleaned?"

He moved closer, his blue eyes reflecting her face. She had gotten lost in those eyes and she wanted to stay lost forever.

"They have to get the bloodstains off the walls," he said, and for a moment she had to think what he was talking about.

"Was it bad?" She looked him over for injury, but couldn't find anything obvious.

"A couple of guys. I had to stop them." His voice was deep and breathless, as if he found it hard to talk.

Her gaze slid from his masculine lips to his wide shoulders. *Okay now, get a grip.*

The man was coming from a fight. This was not the time to jump him.

She stepped back and bumped into a palm tree, glanced around. The restaurant had been transformed into a jungle theme for the ambassador's gala, complete with hundreds of potted palms, orchids blooming on every table and even an artificial stream.

For a moment she had a flashback to the days they'd spent together, what they'd gone through. She had a deeper connection to this man than any other she had known before. And he loved her. The joy of his declaration slammed into her all over again. They'd made it, the danger was over, and he loved her.

"Audrey—" he started to say something, but seemed to change his mind, and instead he kissed her hard on the mouth.

The meeting of their lips was like a switch being thrown—from sanity to insanity in half a second flat. She felt carried away on a mad river that rushed forth wildly, uncontrollable. Reason slipped beyond their reach, and they rode the rolling waters, hanging on to each other.

There were no degrees to the kiss. No tentative brushing of the lips first, no playful nibbles, no slow opening. He took everything at once with a fevered meeting of the tongues.

His hands cupped her face as he drank her, then moved lower, running over her body as thoroughly as if he were taking inventory. And then he reached the bottom of her dress and pulled it above her waist, grounded his hardness into her, bringing moisture to the V of her legs.

Her breath caught at the sudden onslaught of sensations, and she let her head fall against the palm tree, her hands pressed against the solid muscles of his chest. But then she didn't want even that little distance between them and moved her hands to his back, then to his tapered waist, to his firm buttocks. And she pulled him closer still.

He groaned into her mouth, and she felt a tug on her underwear, then it was gone, replaced by his warm hands that caressed her hips and went lower. Her eyes flew open, and as she stared at the crowd outside the restaurant window, she let out a squeal. "Brian!"

He turned his head to see what startled her, looked back, his eyes hooded with passion. "It's mirrored glass. They can't see in."

But reason was gaining a toehold. "What if security comes?"

This was madness. How had they gotten here so fast? How had he cut through all her defenses? She was a mature, reasonable, conservative woman. What happened to making love behind closed doors in a bed?

He nibbled her earlobe as he slipped a finger inside her. "Everybody is on the twenty-third floor. They'll be there for at least another hour."

Pleasure pinged through her and grew, rolling, gathering into an irresistible mass that made her quiver. She reached for his belt and despite her shaking fingers, made pretty quick work of it, pushed his pants and boxers down at the same time, gasped when he sprang free against her belly.

"Look who is happy to see me." She caressed his silky hardness, enjoying the way his eyes darkened, thrilled at the way her touch affected him.

He leaned into her, but the potted palm tree behind her wobbled, too unsteady to hold their combined weight. He lifted her up, her legs wrapped around him, her damp center pressed against his hardness.

Holding her with one hand, he cleared a table with the other and lay her down, holding her legs in place. Then he was inside her with one steady thrust, and took her over and over until she drowned in the pleasure of it and screamed his name.

But he wasn't done with her yet. He was a powerful man and put every bit of that power into use, pleasuring her body, marking every dazed cell of hers as his. It was too much. She couldn't.

Her body felt like a live wire. What he did to her seemed unreal, impossible. But she felt tension build deep inside her once again, and when he finally poured his hot seed into her, his body shuddering, a deep groan torn from his chest, she sank into yet another wave of pleasure.

He didn't pull out, but instead lifted her

and moved back, sat on the floor with her still on his lap, leaning his back against a giant potted palm, resting his forehead against hers.

Then after a while, when their breathing evened, he looked up and smiled.

"What?"

"You have orchid blossoms in your hair."

"I've gone native." She smiled back at him.

He nodded. "You certainly have."

Then his expression grew more serious. "Audrey, this is not why I came back…." He fell silent as if looking for the right words.

"I'm glad just the same that we got around to it." She grinned.

"You know, when I got you away from Omar's camp, I thought I was rescuing you, but I think at the end, you ended up rescuing me."

Her heart flipped over from the way he was looking at her. "We rescued each other."

He brushed his lips against hers, then pulled back. "You take away my reason. I tried to fight it. I'm not a hundred percent convinced this is the right thing for you. But I love you like mad, there's no help for it. It's like malaria. Once it gets into the blood, there's no getting it out." He glanced away, then back at her again. "I need to ask you a question."

She nodded.

"Who is Josh to you?" His face was as serious as she'd ever seen it.

"My ex-husband," she responded, unsure what that had to do with anything.

He put his hand over her heart. "Who is he here?"

It took less than a second to come up with a response. "Nobody."

He hugged her so fiercely, she could scarcely breathe.

"You've been worrying about that?" He had to be kidding.

"I'm a man with no family, no job, no home—very little to recommend me, really. But I'm a hard worker and I'm scared of little. I would work like hell to make a good life for us if you agreed to share yours with me. I know there are a hundred men out there who'd be better for you, could offer you more, but nobody on this earth could love you more than I. Can you give me a chance?"

She blinked the tears back from her eyes. "Yes," she said, and threw her arms around him. "If you can give *us* a chance. I have a daughter. We come as a package deal."

His reply came slowly. "It's almost too good to believe. I would love nothing more. I never pictured—but I might never again be the man I once was." He pulled back and searched her eyes. "My father, after the war he was different. He could never find his way back. I don't know if I can."

She smoothed the furrow from his forehead. "I fell in love with the man you are now."

His beautiful blue eyes sparkled with emotion. "Can you say that again?"

"I love you, Brian Welkins."

He held her tight, and she felt him harden inside her.

She grinned. Was he for real? "Making up for time lost, are we?"

"I'm all uncivilized. See what you'll have to put up with?"

"I like uncivilized," she said and rotated her hips. "I think I developed a taste for the wild and untamed."

He grinned, sudden relief flooding his face, followed by a look of mischief, and pushed in deeper. "Prepare for jungle heat."

Epilogue

He couldn't wait to get there and hold that little baby in his hands. Brian picked up the suitcases. Wow. What had she packed, iron ore? Then he heard a faint clinking—jars of baby food.

"Are you sure you're ready for this?"

He smiled at Audrey and Mei. "More than sure."

"You're not going to feel outnumbered? Some men would say three women in one house are too many."

"They don't know my girls." He winked at her. "You can never have too much love. I can't wait to see our new baby."

"I'm crazy about you," Audrey said.

As always, the simple declaration took

his breath away. To have her, Mei and another baby soon was such an unexpected and humbling blessing.

"You have the adoption papers?"

"Right here." He patted his left inner pocket.

"It will be perfect, you know, them being so close in age." Audrey grabbed the diaper bag.

"They'll be like you and Nicky." He grinned. "We'll have to give them some little brothers to keep them on their toes." He was looking forward to having a large family.

"We have to stop by Nicky's. I forgot to drop off the key so she can come and water the orchids." She grabbed the dropping pacifier with the reflexes of a seasoned soldier, and pushed it back between Mei's rosy lips before the baby even missed it. "Business is taken care of?"

God, he loved them. He nodded. "Some old buddies of mine are going to take over while we're gone."

The business he'd built in the past year was thriving, offering survival-type team-building retreats to major corporations. He enjoyed his small company, founded with the $500,000 reward from the Malaysian government that had been the bounty on Omar's head. They had Hamid in custody, too. And since Brian had been instrumental in the guerilla leader's capture, he was going to get yet another reward. But even without it, his business brought in more than enough.

The work made him feel useful, providing him with enough that was familiar so that he felt comfortable stretching and trying new angles. He'd been a soldier once, then a prisoner, reduced to the level of a wild animal. But neither of those things defined him now.

Mei spit the pacifier half-across the room and reached her chubby little hands toward him. "Da-da," she said.

And he smiled, because that's exactly what he was. Father to the sweetest little girl, husband to the most exceptional woman. The past didn't matter. He was what he made of himself with his new family.

"Let's go then." Audrey took a last glance

at the house. "We better not miss the plane."

"It's kind of fitting that we'll celebrate our first wedding anniversary in KL."

"Very." She gave him a quick kiss, then winked. "Hope we'll get a chance to sneak into the jungle."

"Count on it, wife." He recaptured her lips and deepened the kiss.

e♦HARLEQUIN.com

The Ultimate Destination for Women's Fiction

Visit eHarlequin.com's Bookstore today
for today's most popular books at great prices.

- An extensive selection of romance books by top authors!

- Choose our convenient "bill me" option. No credit card required.

- New releases, Themed Collections and hard-to-find backlist.

- A sneak peek at upcoming books.

- Check out book excerpts, book summaries and Reader Recommendations from other members and post your own too.

- Find out what everybody's reading in Bestsellers.

- Save BIG with everyday discounts and exclusive online offers!

- Our Category Legend will help you select reading that's exactly right for you!

- Visit our Bargain Outlet often for huge savings and special offers!

- Sweepstakes offers. Enter for your chance to win special prizes, autographed books and more.

**Your purchases are 100%
guaranteed—so shop online
at www.eHarlequin.com today!**

INTBB104R

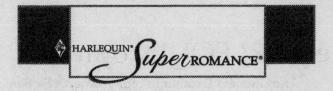
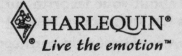

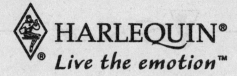
HARLEQUIN®
Live the emotion™

SILHOUETTE Romance

From first love to forever, these love stories
are fairy tale romances for today's woman.

Silhouette Desire

Modern, passionate reads that are powerful and provocative.

Silhouette SPECIAL EDITION™

Emotional, compelling stories that capture the intensity
of living, loving and creating a family in today's world.

Silhouette INTIMATE MOMENTS™

A roller-coaster read that delivers romantic thrills
in a world of suspense, adventure and more.